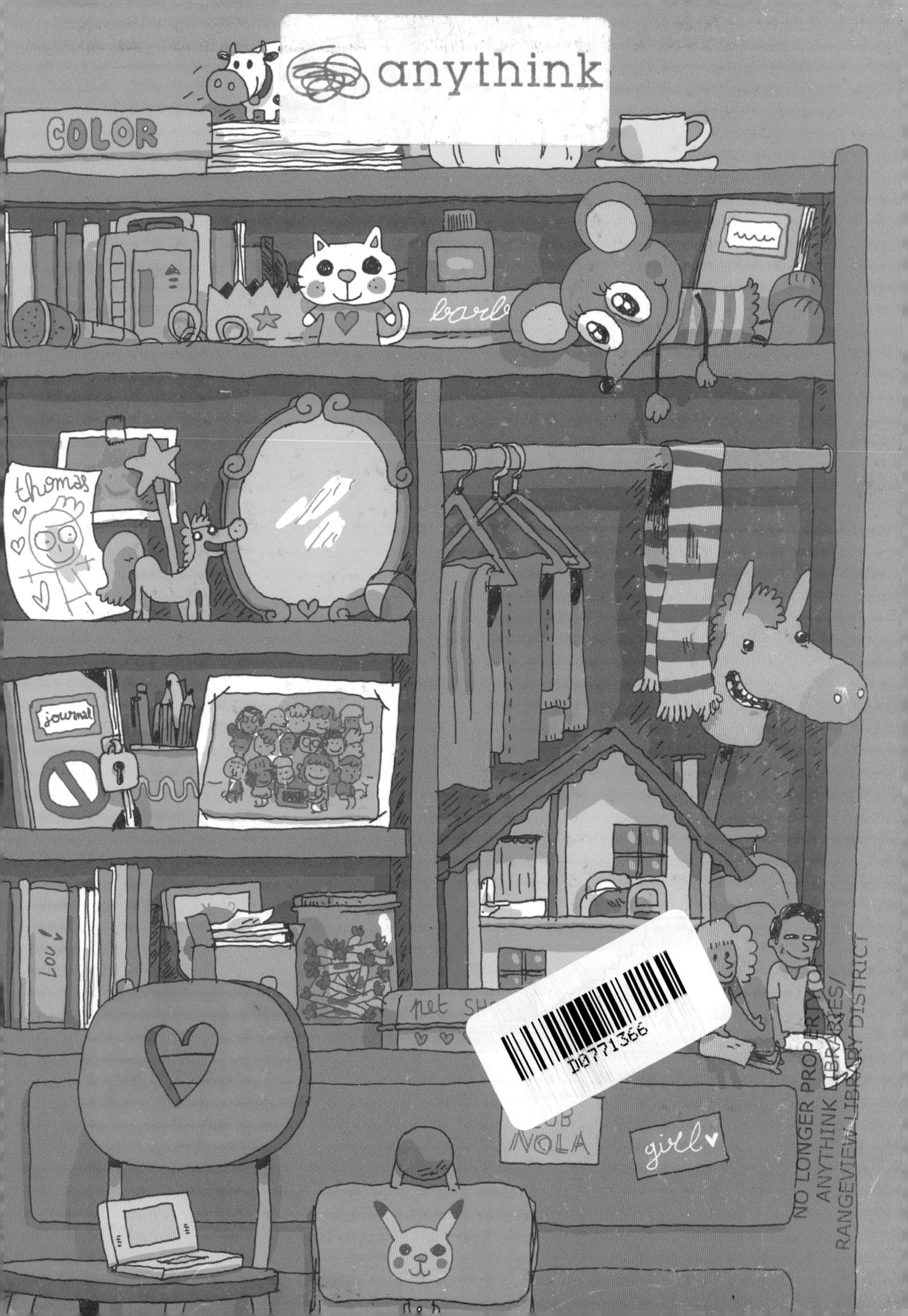
COLOR
thomas
journal
Lou!
girl

Where's Leopold? 1

Your Pajamas Are Showing!

by Michel-Yves Schmitt

illustrated by Vincent Caut

Graphic Universe™ • Minneapolis • New York

For Eliott and his mom. Thank you to Martin for his confidence from the beginning of this adventure

—Michel-Yves

A big thank-you to Michel-Yves, Martin, and to everyone who will read this book

—Vincent

Story by Michel-Yves Schmitt
Art by Vincent Caut
Translation by Carol Klio Burrell

English translation copyright © 2013 by Lerner Publishing Group, Inc.

First American edition published in 2013 by Graphic Universe™.
Published by arrangement with MEDIATOON LICENSING—France.

Où es-tu Léopold?
1/On voit ton pyjama!
© DUPUIS 2011—Caut & Schmitt
www.dupuis.com

Graphic Universe™
A division of Lerner Publishing Group, Inc.
241 First Avenue North
Minneapolis, MN 55401 U.S.A.

Website address: www.lernerbooks.com

Library of Congress Cataloging-in-Publication Data

Schmitt, Michel-Yves.
   [On voit ton pyjama! English]
   Your pajamas are showing! / written by Michel-Yves Schmitt ; illustrated by Vincent Caut. — 1st American ed.
      p.   cm. — (Where's Leopold? ; #1)
   ISBN 978–1–4677–0769–5 (lib. bdg. : alk. paper)
   1. Graphic novels. [1. Graphic novels. 2. Invisibility—Fiction. 3. Brothers and sisters—Fiction.] I. Caut, Vincent, ill. II. Title.
PZ7.7.S37 2013
741.5'944—dc23   2012021660

Manufactured in the United States of America
1 – BP – 12/31/12

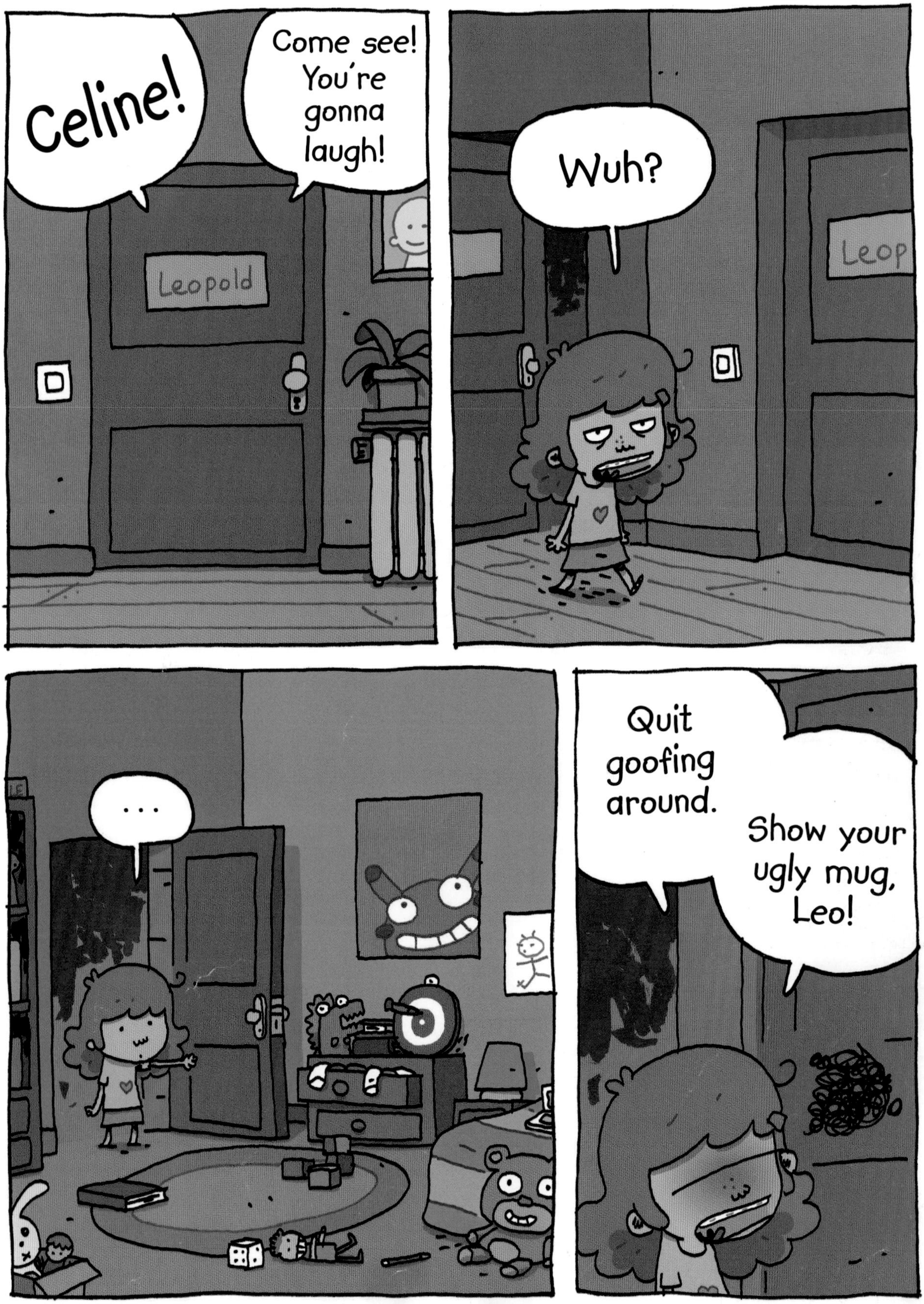
Celine!
Come see! You're gonna laugh!
Leopold
Wuh?
Leop
...
Quit goofing around.
Show your ugly mug, Leo!

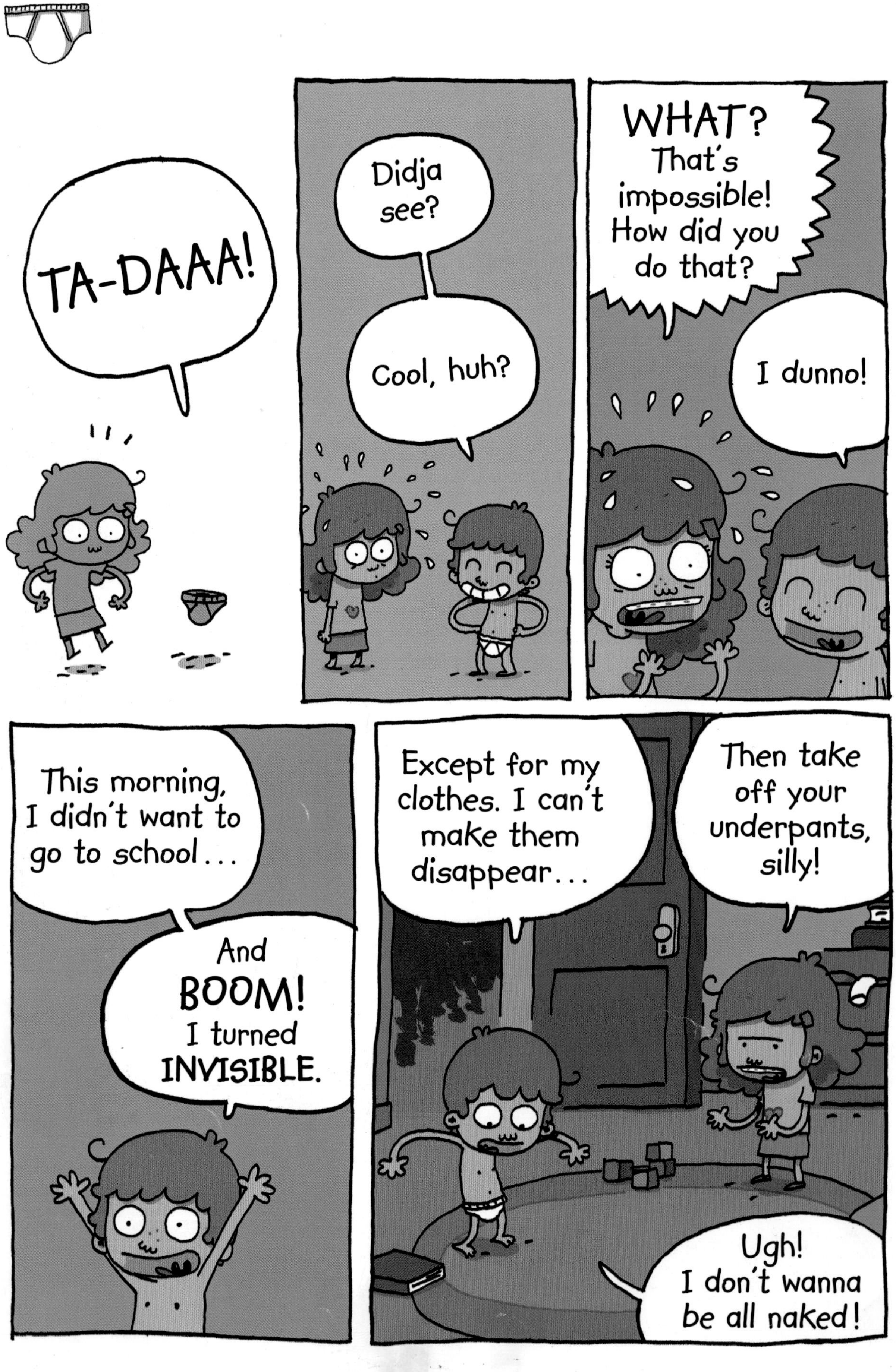
TA-DAAA!
Didja see?
Cool, huh?
WHAT? That's impossible! How did you do that?
I dunno!
This morning, I didn't want to go to school...
And BOOM! I turned INVISIBLE.
Except for my clothes. I can't make them disappear...
Then take off your underpants, silly!
Ugh! I don't wanna be all naked!

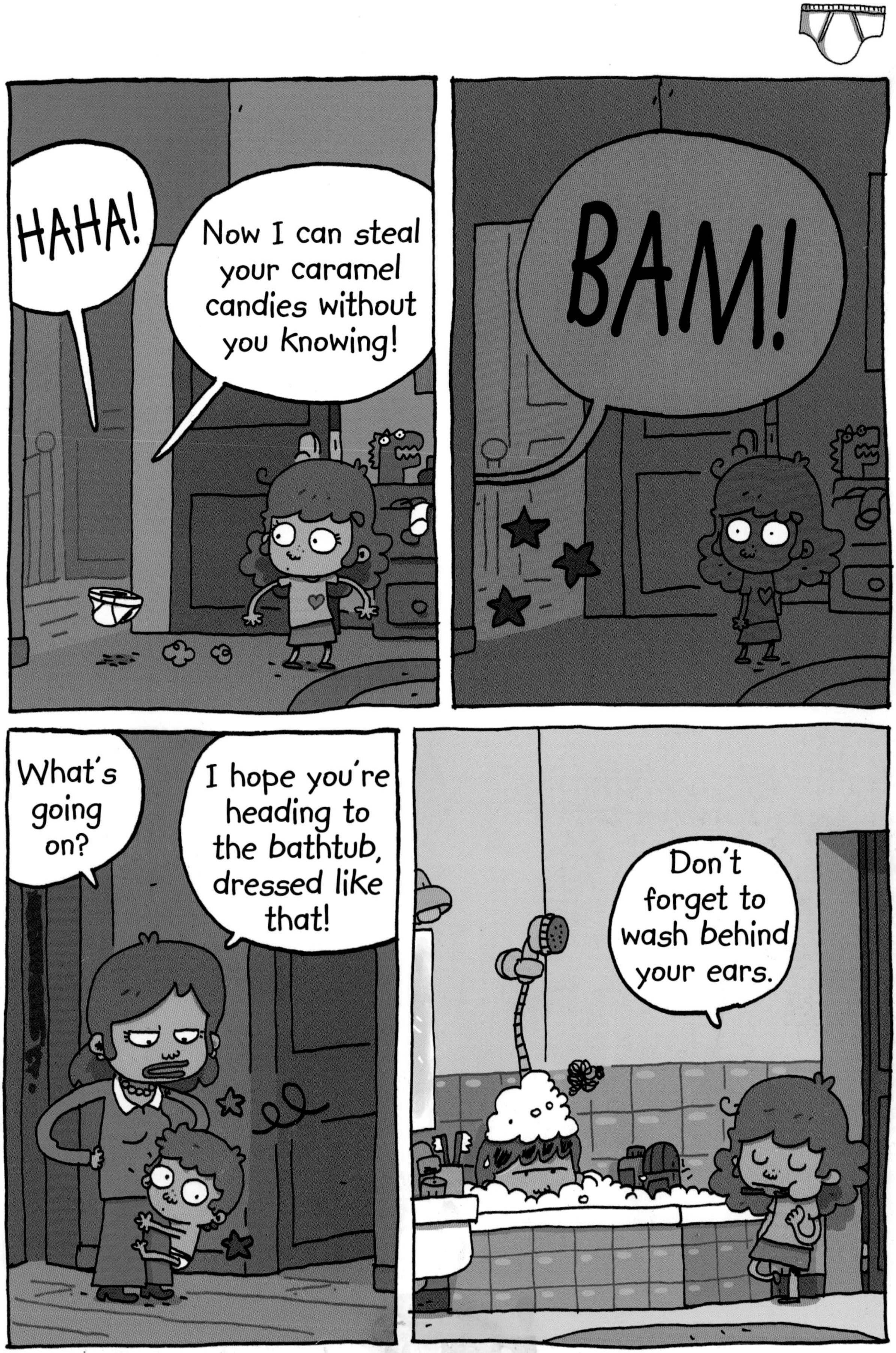
HAHA!
Now I can steal your caramel candies without you knowing!
BAM!
What's going on?
I hope you're heading to the bathtub, dressed like that!
Don't forget to wash behind your ears.

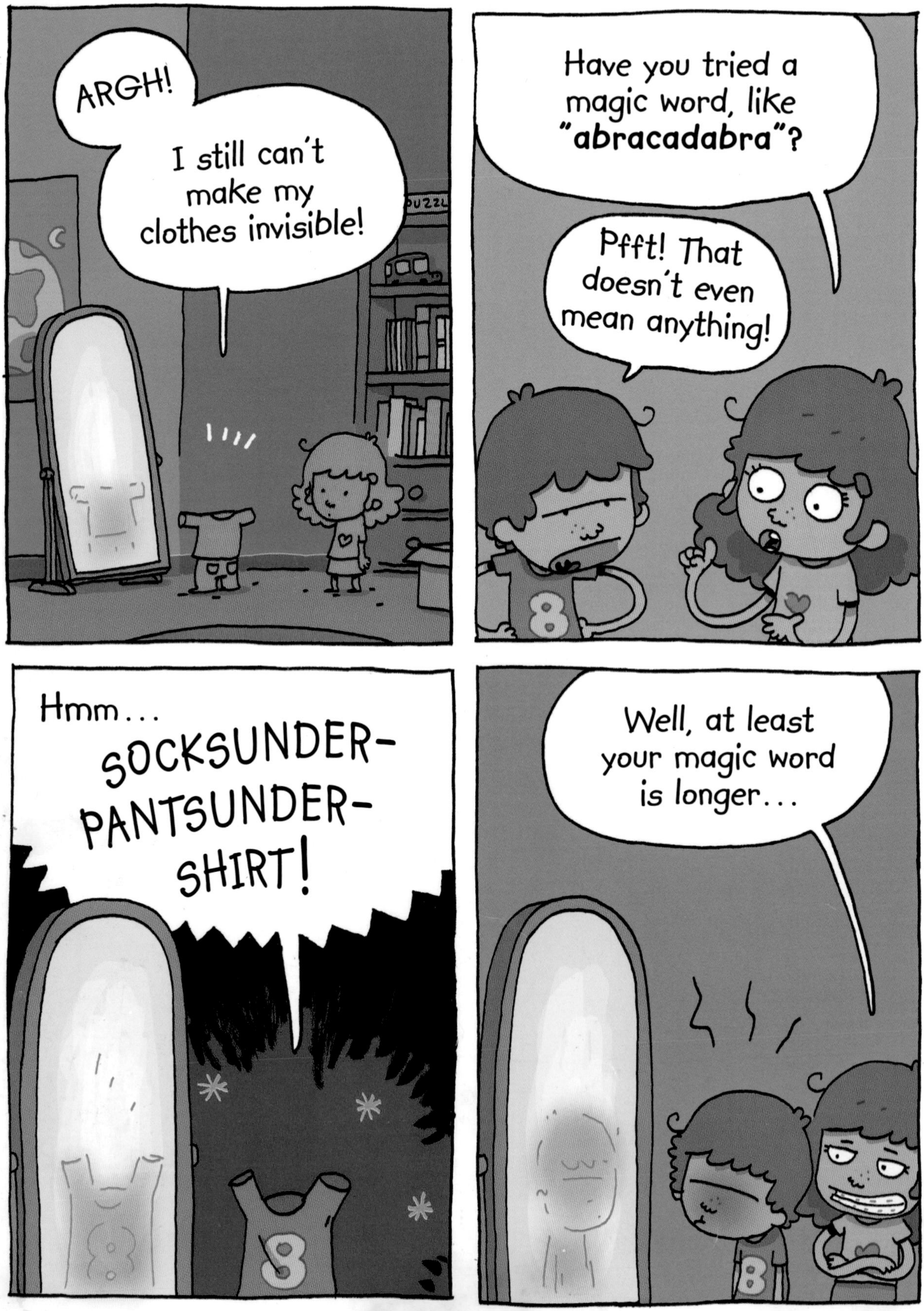
ARGH!
I still can't make my clothes invisible!
Have you tried a magic word, like **"abracadabra"**?
Pfft! That doesn't even mean anything!
Hmm...
SOCKSUNDER-PANTSUNDER-SHIRT!
Well, at least your magic word is longer...

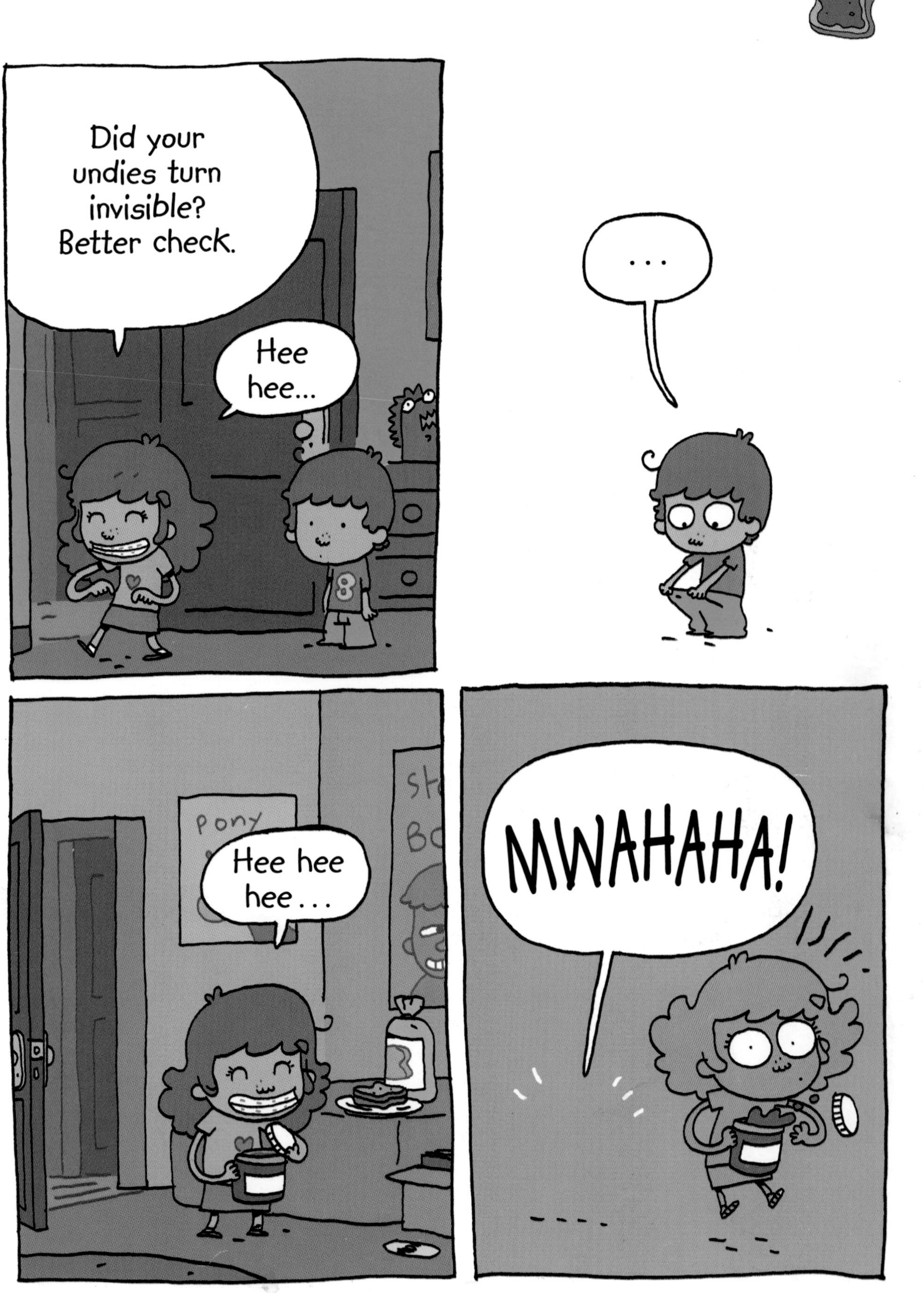
Did your undies turn invisible? Better check.
Hee hee...
. . .
Pony
Hee hee hee . . .
MWAHAHA!

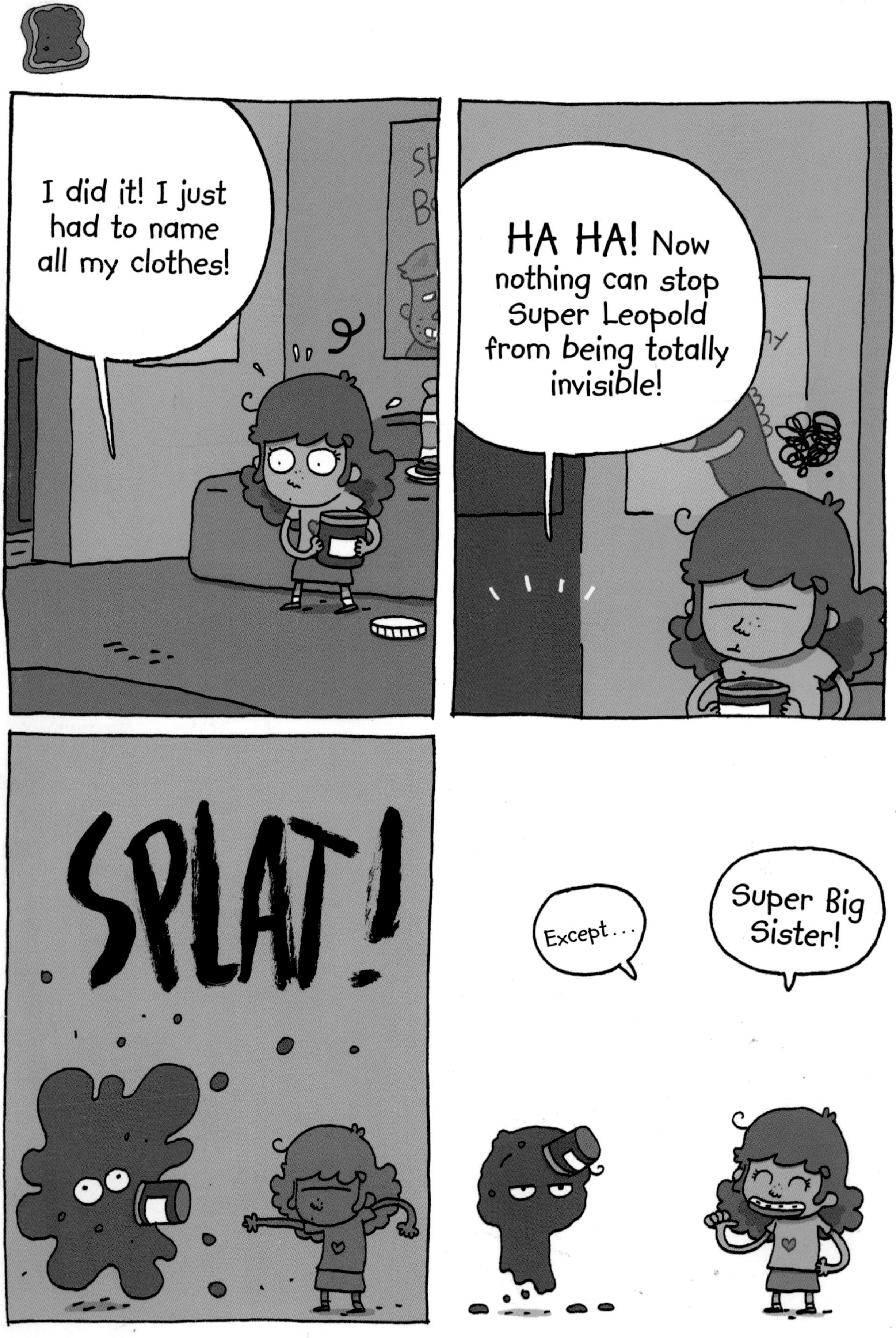
I did it! I just had to name all my clothes!
HA HA! Now nothing can stop Super Leopold from being totally invisible!
SPLAT!
Except...
Super Big Sister!

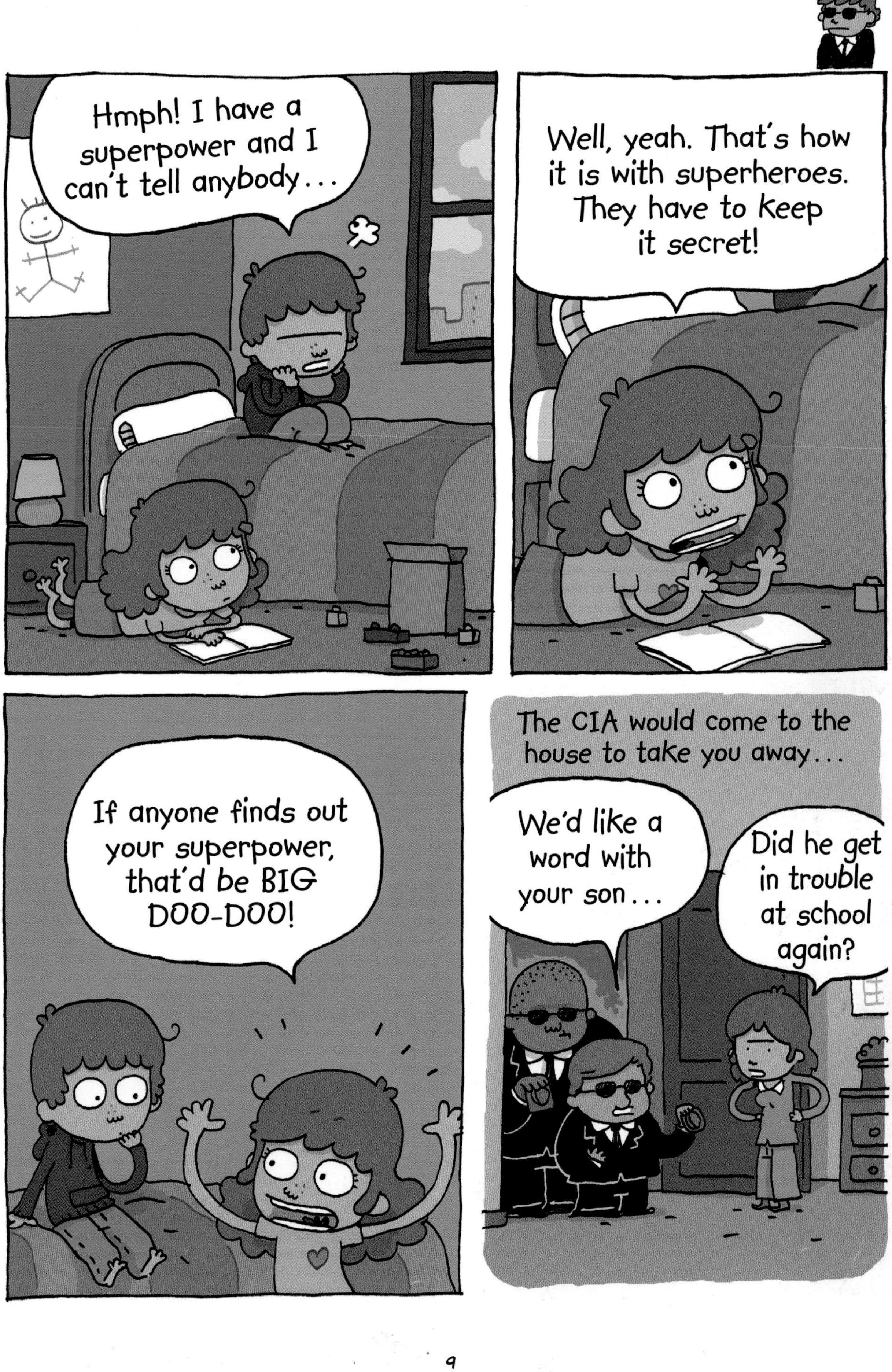
Hmph! I have a superpower and I can't tell anybody . . .
Well, yeah. That's how it is with superheroes. They have to keep it secret!
If anyone finds out your superpower, that'd be BIG DOO-DOO!
The CIA would come to the house to take you away . . .
We'd like a word with your son . . .
Did he get in trouble at school again?

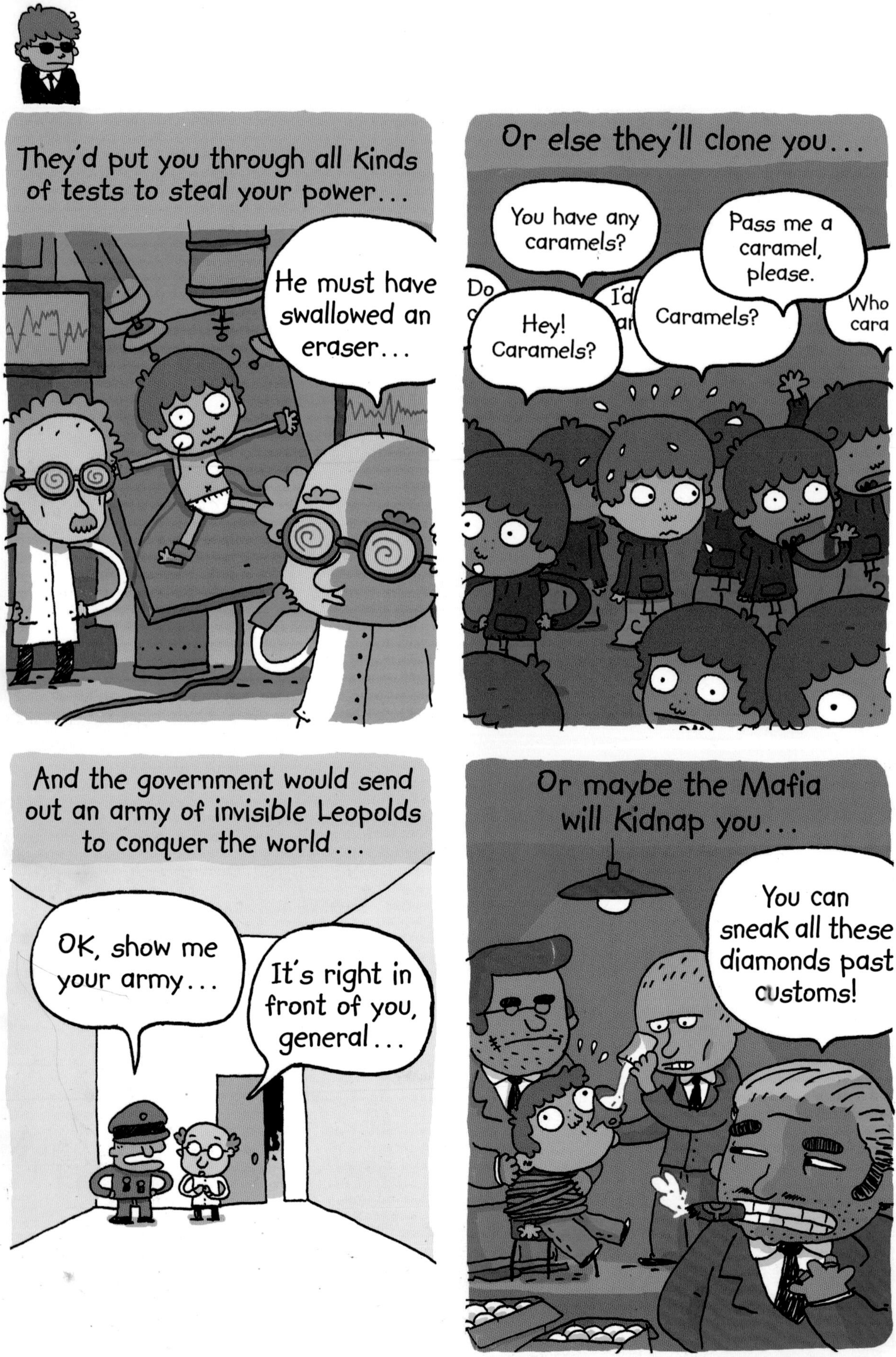
They'd put you through all kinds of tests to steal your power...
He must have swallowed an eraser...
Or else they'll clone you...
You have any caramels?
Pass me a caramel, please.
Hey! Caramels?
Caramels?
And the government would send out an army of invisible Leopolds to conquer the world...
OK, show me your army...
It's right in front of you, general...
Or maybe the Mafia will kidnap you...
You can sneak all these diamonds past customs!

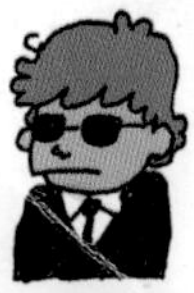

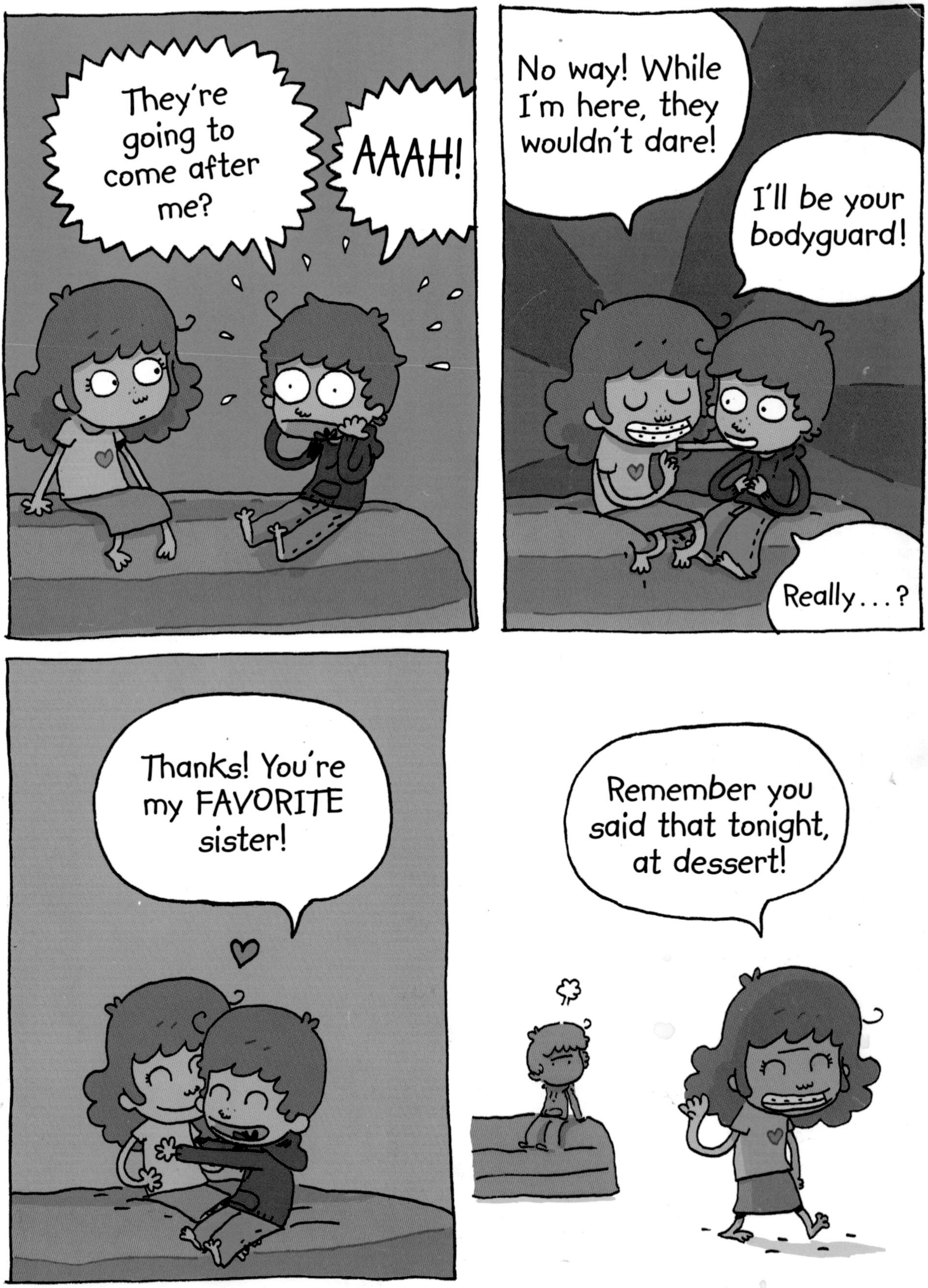
They're going to come after me?
AAAH!
No way! While I'm here, they wouldn't dare!
I'll be your bodyguard!
Really . . . ?
Thanks! You're my FAVORITE sister!
Remember you said that tonight, at dessert!

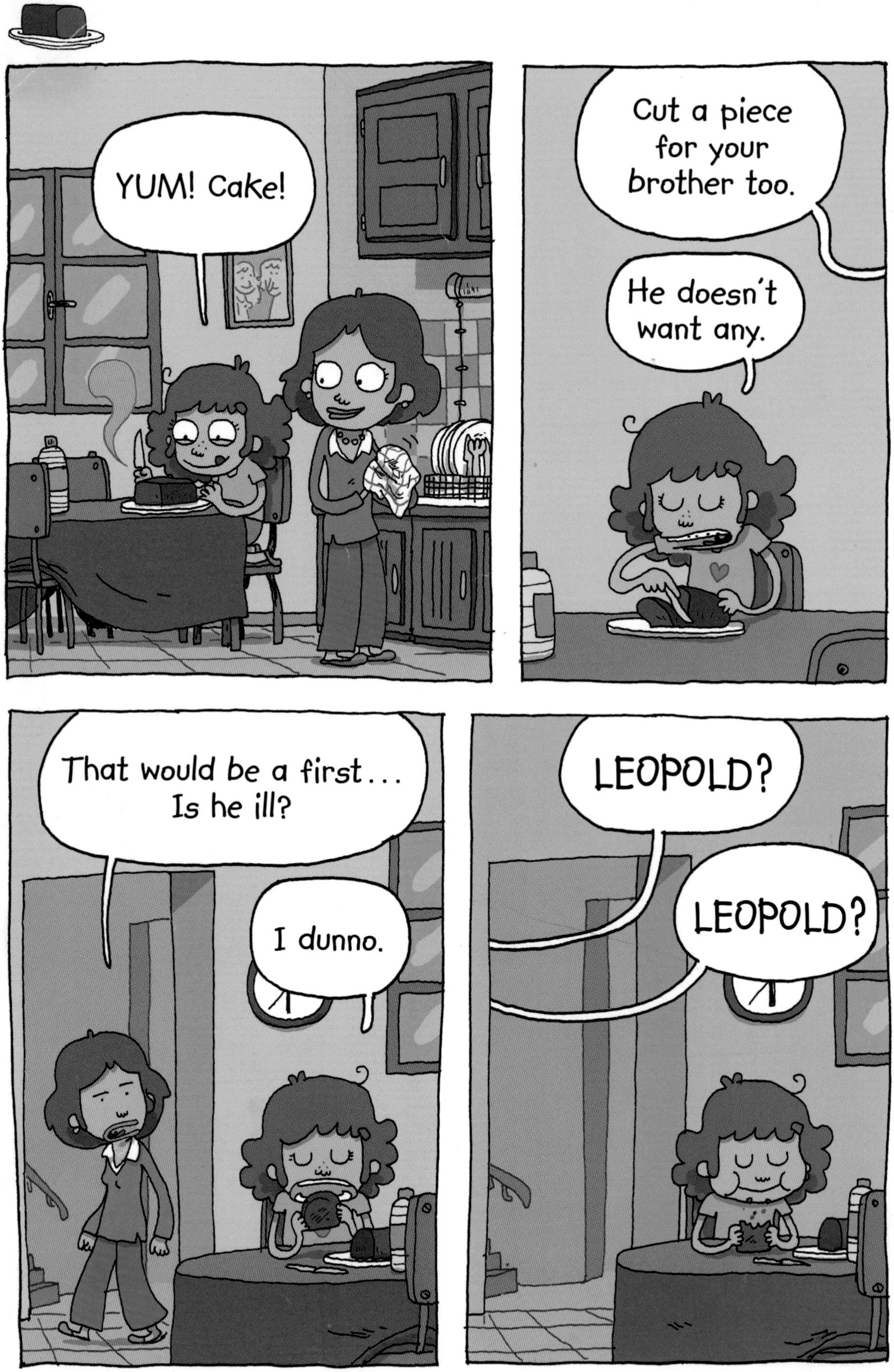
YUM! Cake!
Cut a piece for your brother too.
He doesn't want any.
That would be a first... Is he ill?
I dunno.
LEOPOLD?
LEOPOLD?

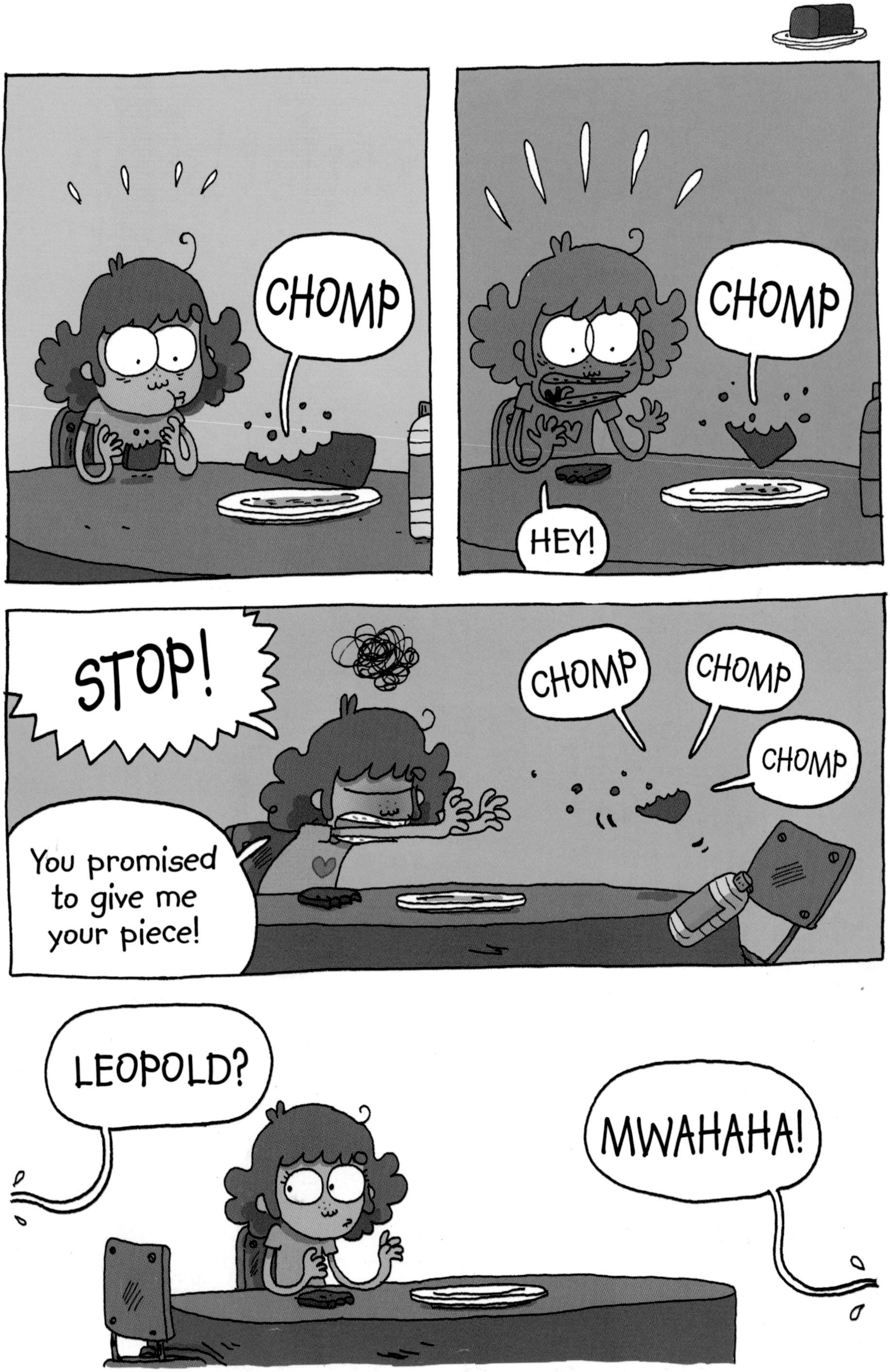
CHOMP
CHOMP
HEY!
STOP!
CHOMP
CHOMP
CHOMP
You promised to give me your piece!
LEOPOLD?
MWAHAHA!

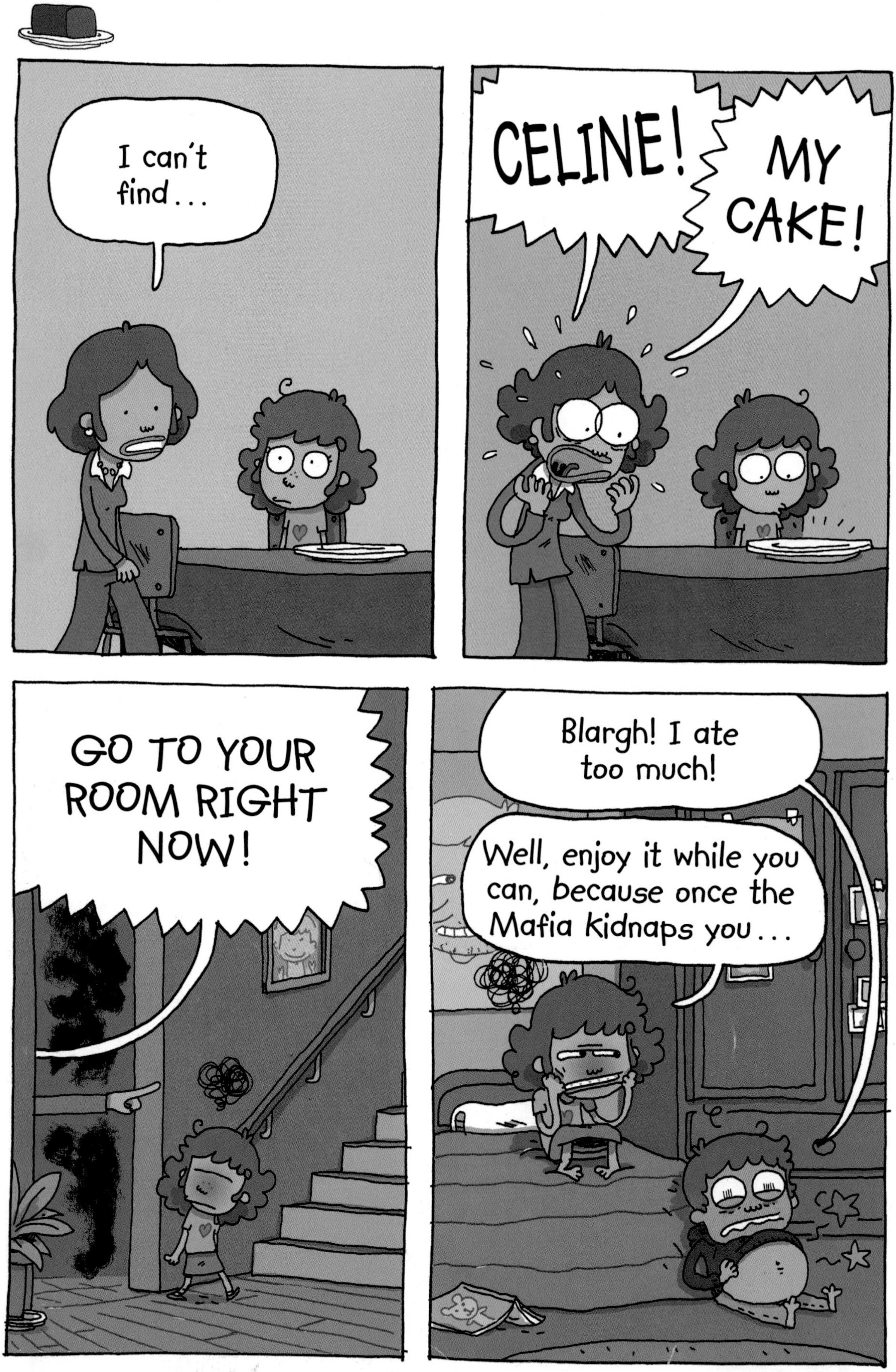
I can't find...
CELINE!
MY CAKE!
GO TO YOUR ROOM RIGHT NOW!
Blargh! I ate too much!
Well, enjoy it while you can, because once the Mafia kidnaps you...

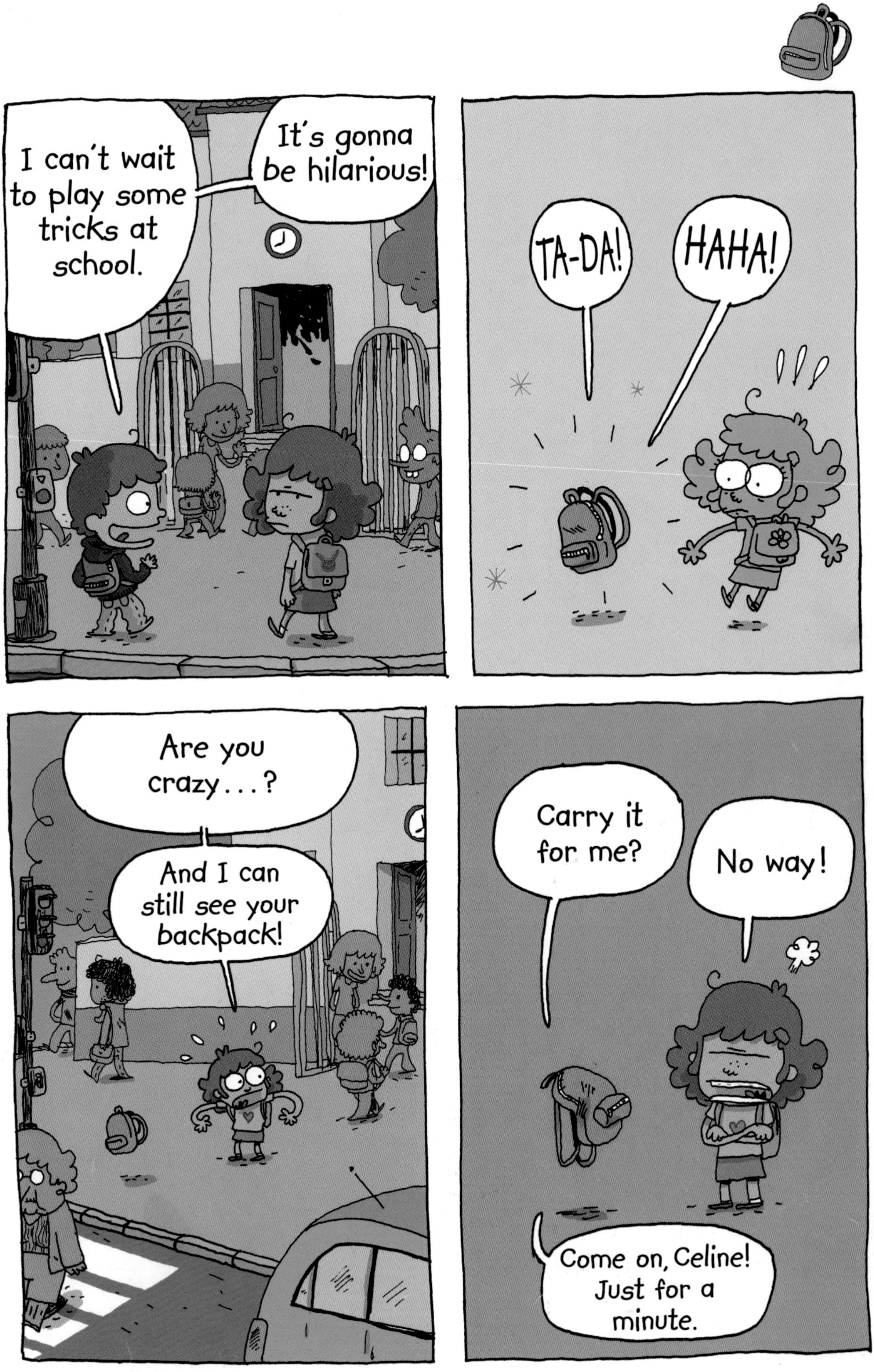
I can't wait to play some tricks at school.
It's gonna be hilarious!
TA-DA!
HAHA!
Are you crazy...?
And I can still see your backpack!
Carry it for me?
No way!
Come on, Celine! Just for a minute.

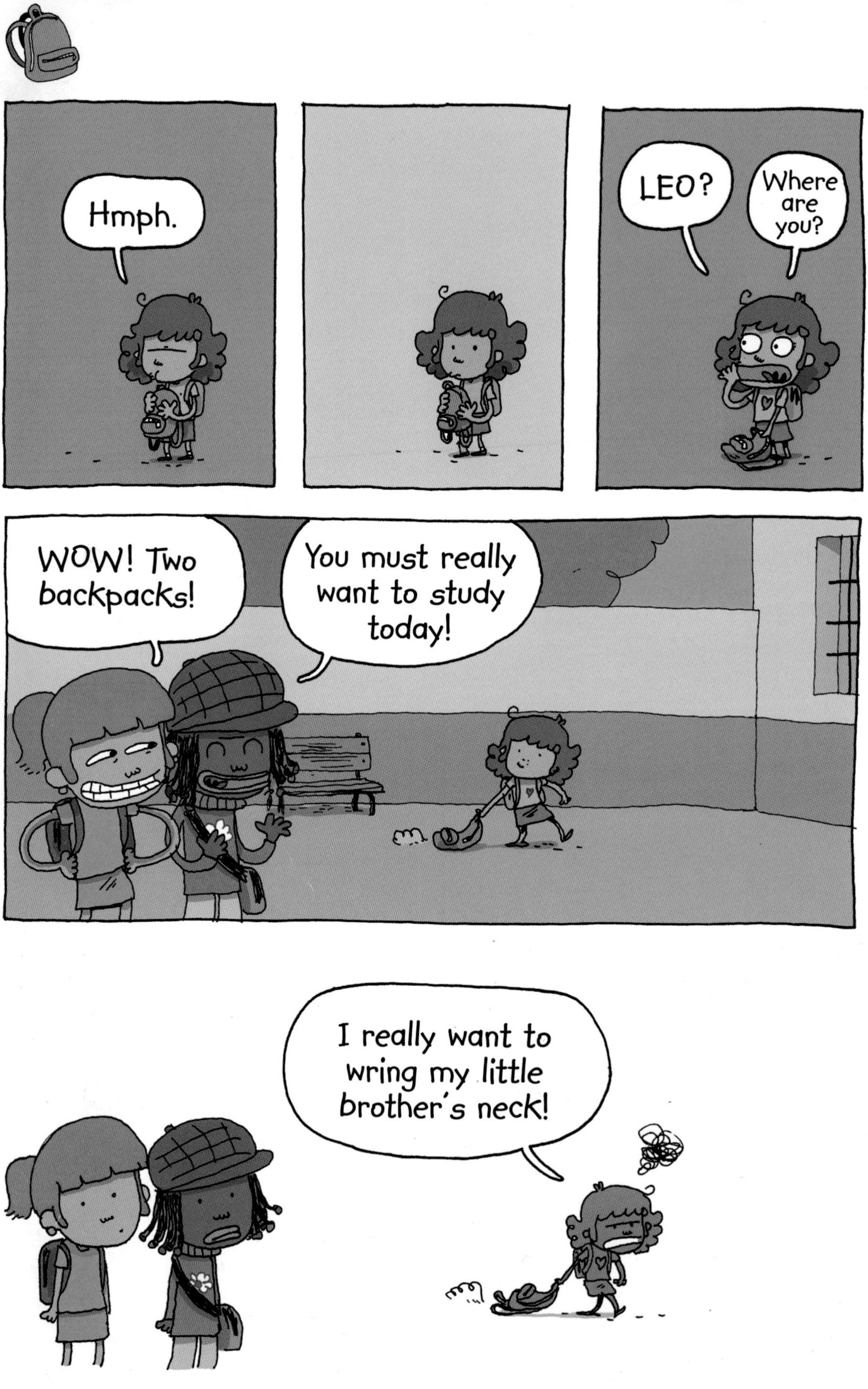
Hmph.
LEO?
Where are you?
WOW! Two backpacks!
You must really want to study today!
I really want to wring my little brother's neck!

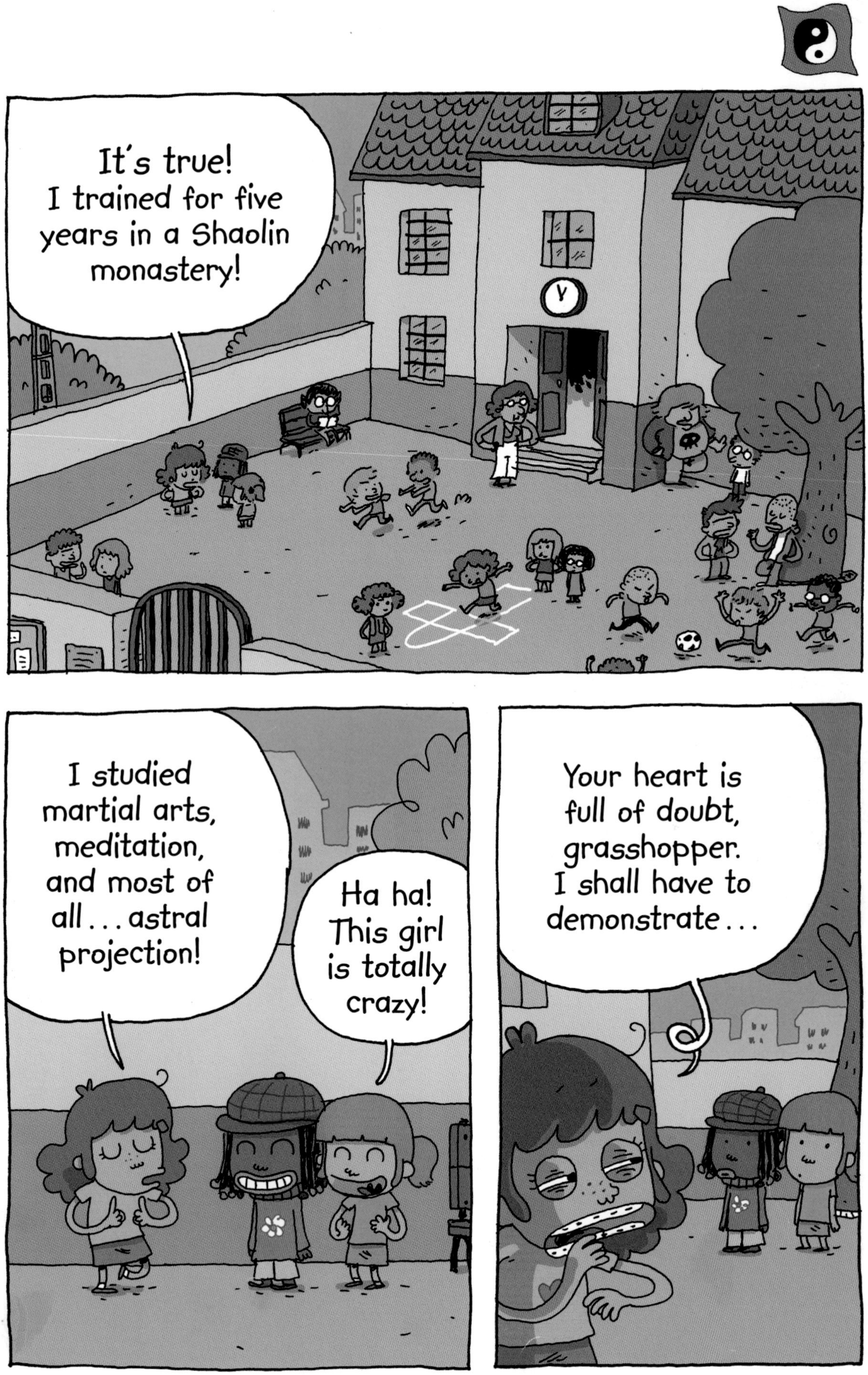
It's true!
I trained for five years in a Shaolin monastery!
I studied martial arts, meditation, and most of all . . . astral projection!
Ha ha! This girl is totally crazy!
Your heart is full of doubt, grasshopper. I shall have to demonstrate . . .

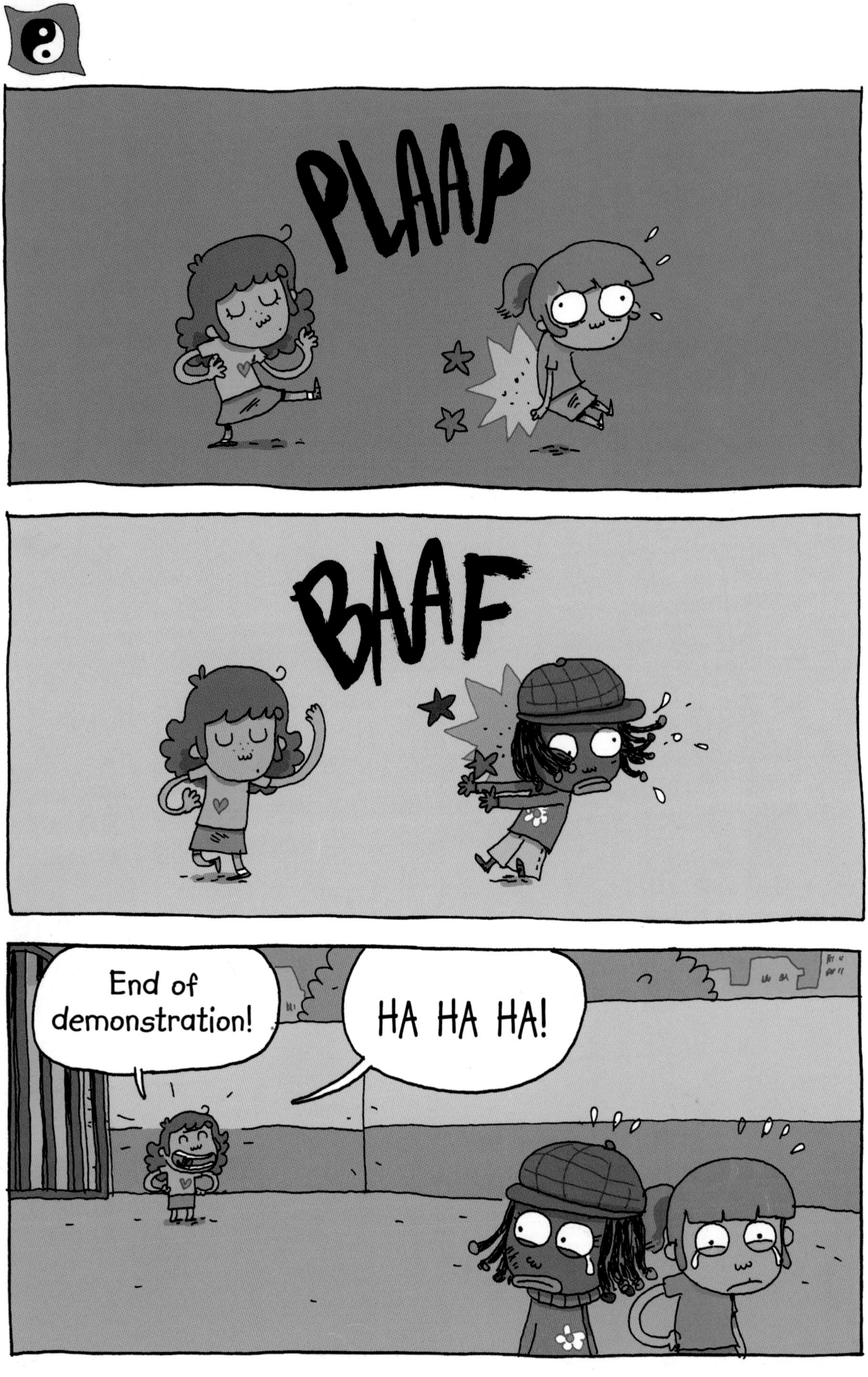
PLAAP
BAAF
End of demonstration!
HA HA HA!

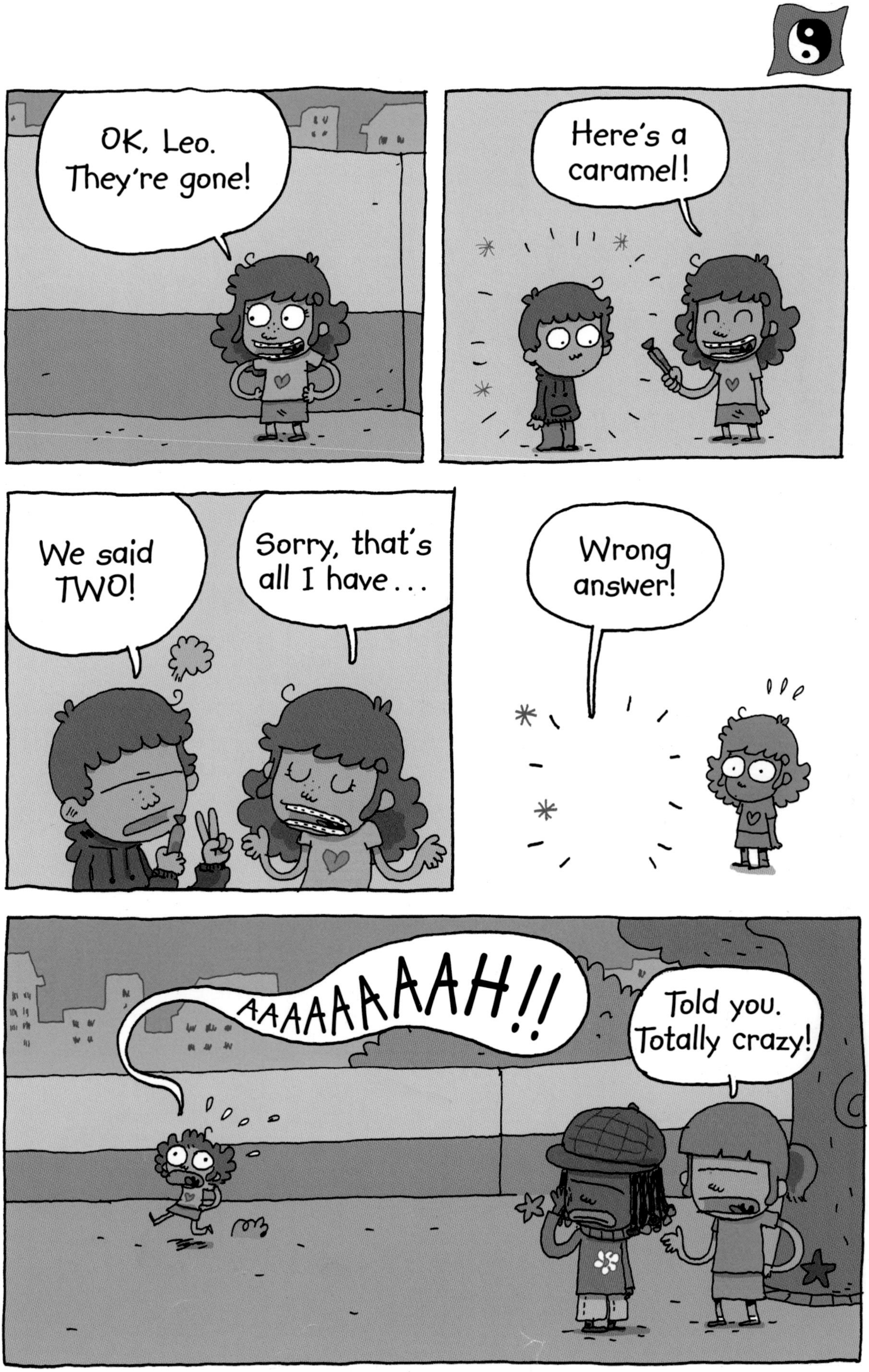
OK, Leo.
They're gone!
Here's a caramel!
We said TWO!
Sorry, that's all I have...
Wrong answer!
AAAAAAAAH!!
Told you.
Totally crazy!

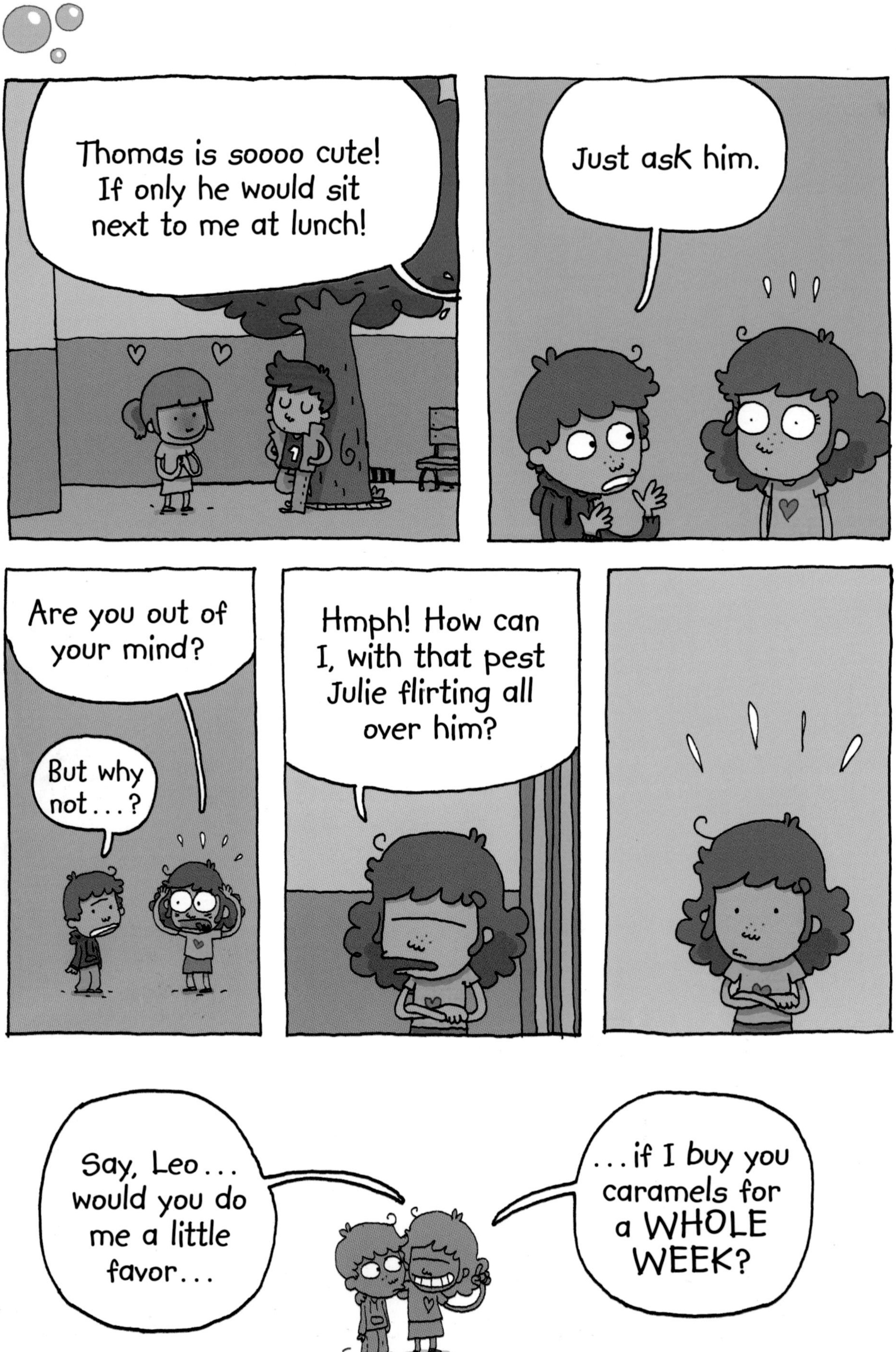
Thomas is soooo cute! If only he would sit next to me at lunch!
Just ask him.
Are you out of your mind?
But why not...?
Hmph! How can I, with that pest Julie flirting all over him?
Say, Leo... would you do me a little favor...
...if I buy you caramels for a WHOLE WEEK?

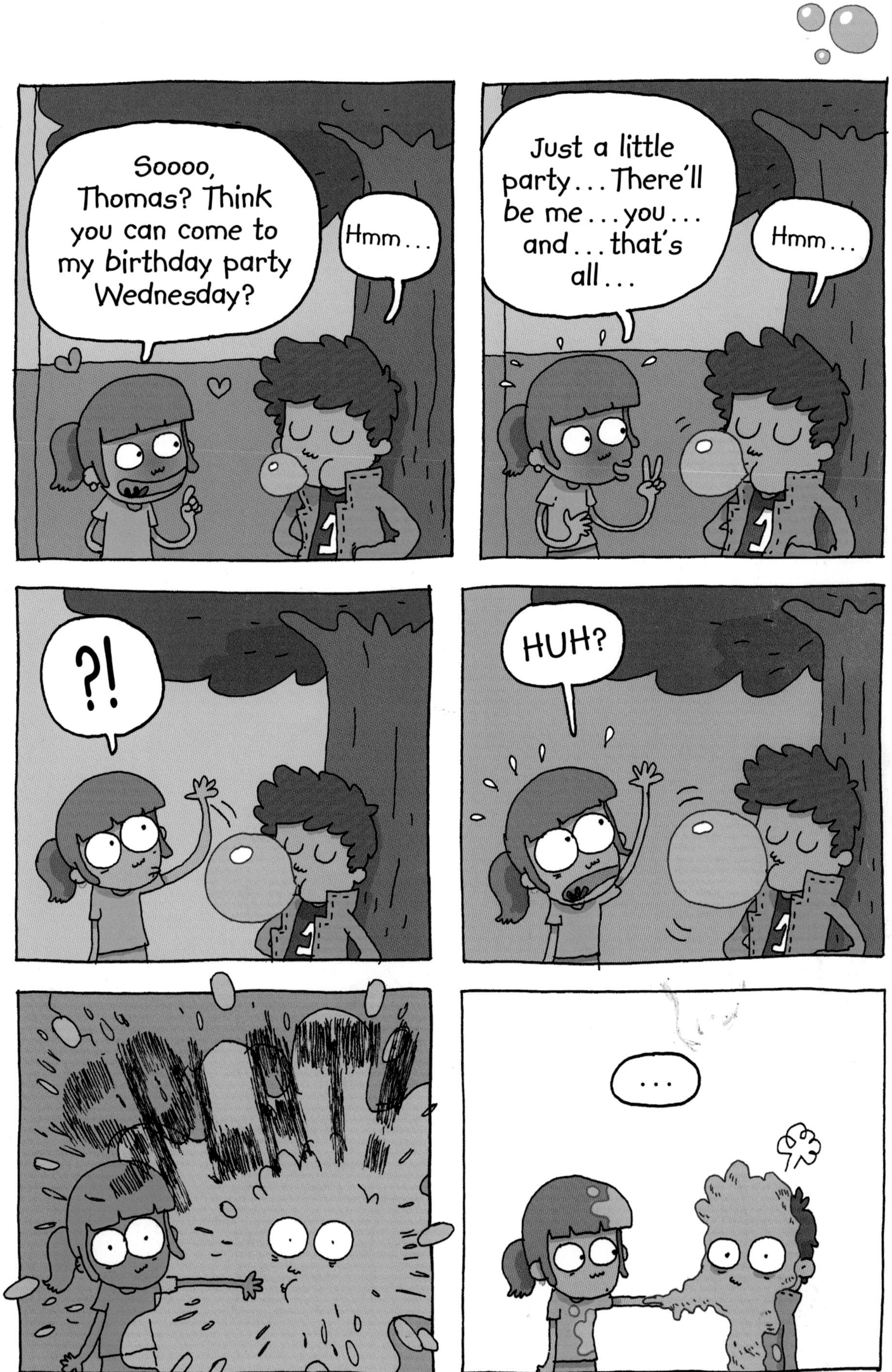
Soooo, Thomas? Think you can come to my birthday party Wednesday?
Hmm . . .
Just a little party . . . There'll be me . . . you . . . and . . . that's all . . .
Hmm . . .
?!
HUH?
SPLAT!
. . .

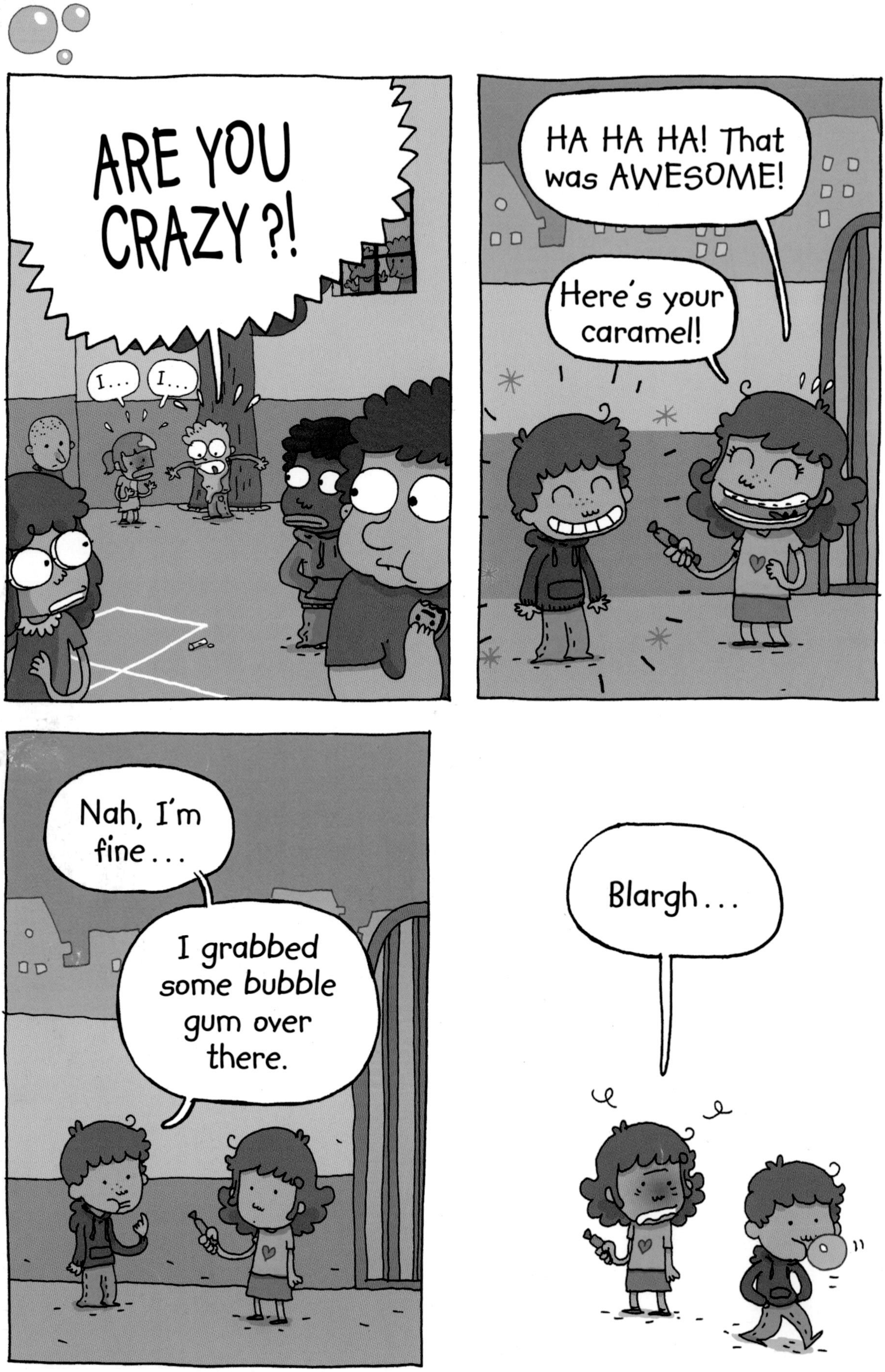
ARE YOU CRAZY ?!
I...
I...
HA HA HA! That was AWESOME!
Here's your caramel!
Nah, I'm fine...
I grabbed some bubble gum over there.
Blargh...

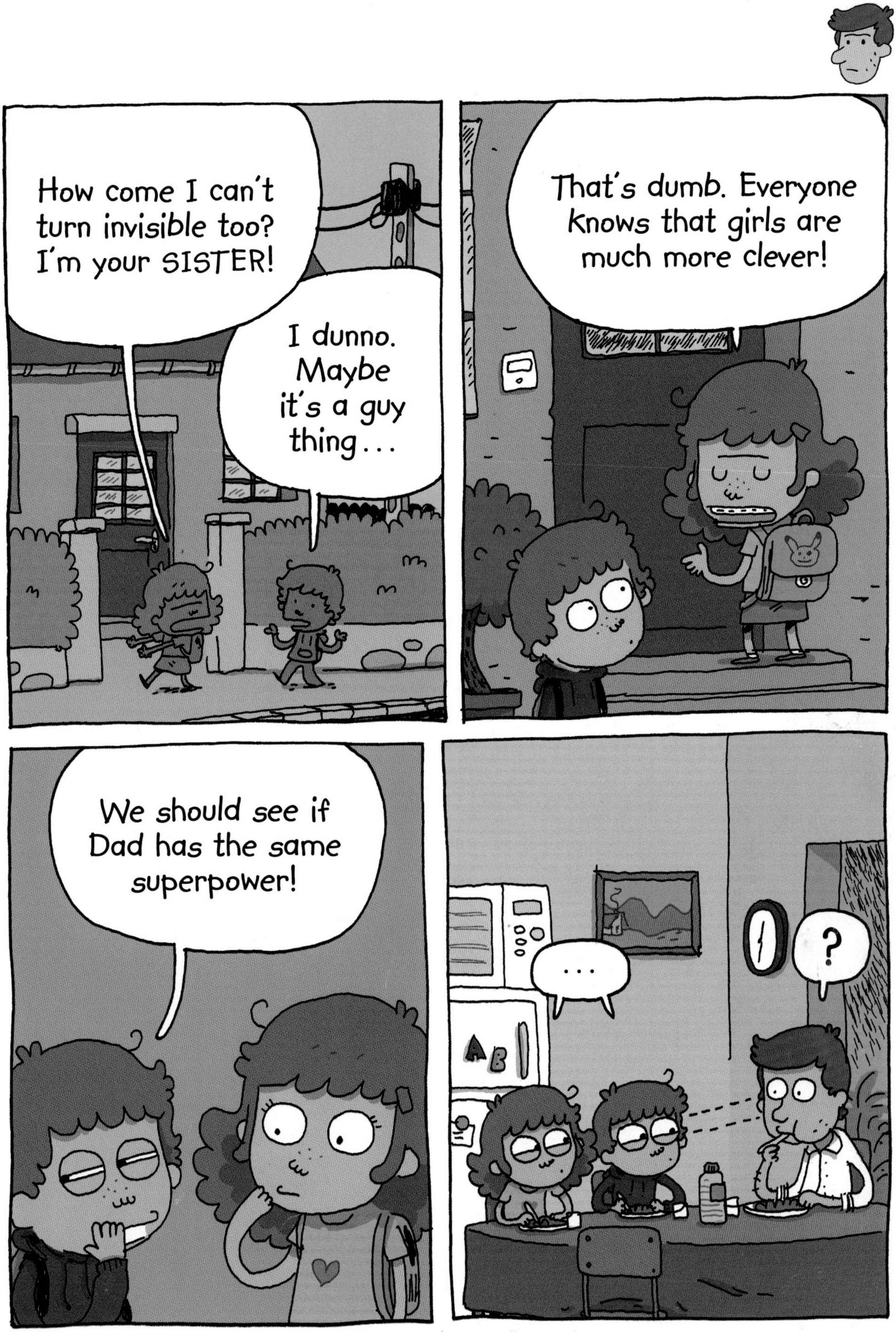
How come I can't turn invisible too? I'm your SISTER!
I dunno. Maybe it's a guy thing...
That's dumb. Everyone knows that girls are much more clever!
We should see if Dad has the same superpower!
...
?

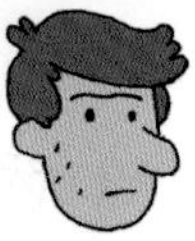

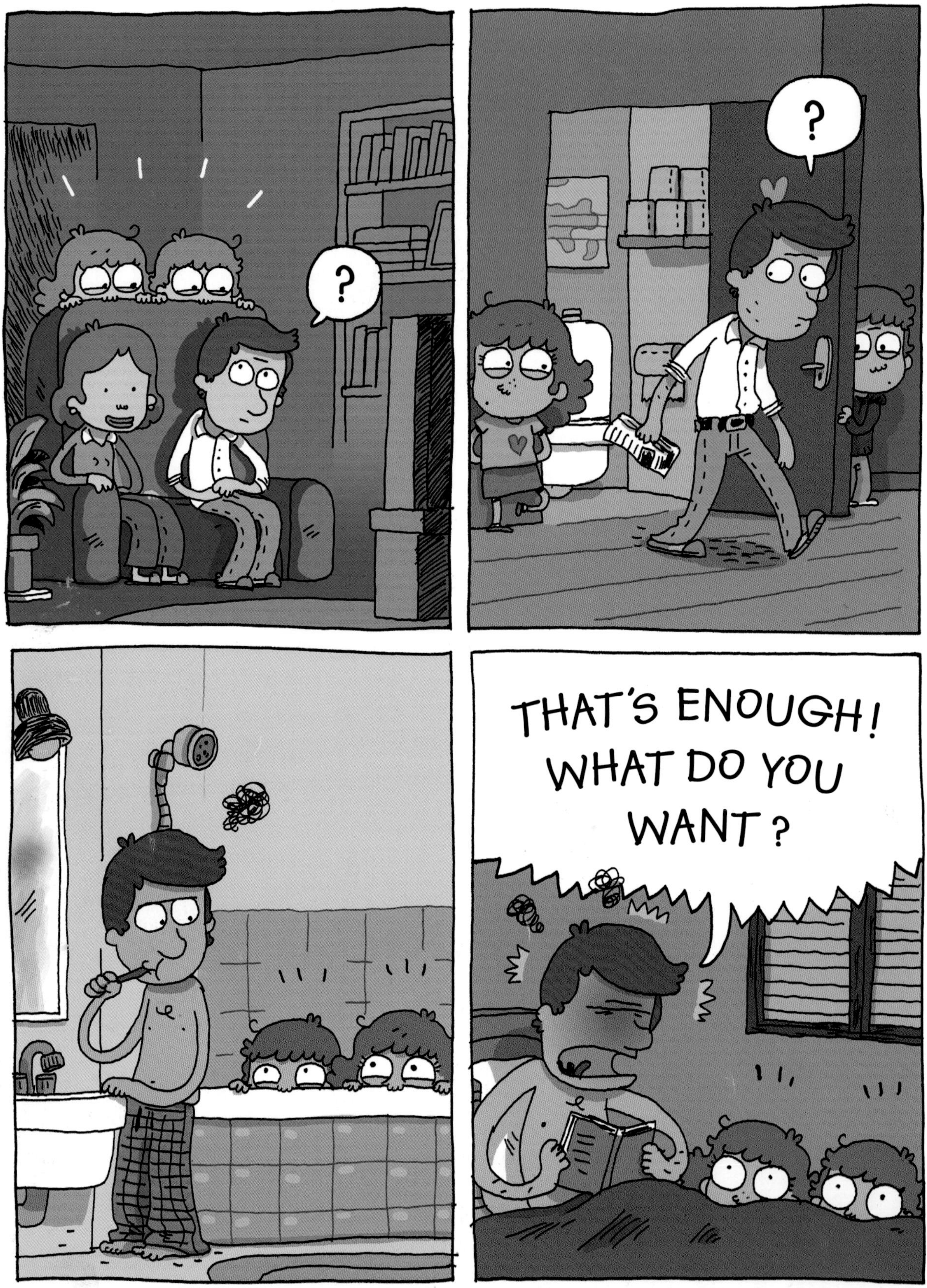
?
?
THAT'S ENOUGH! WHAT DO YOU WANT?

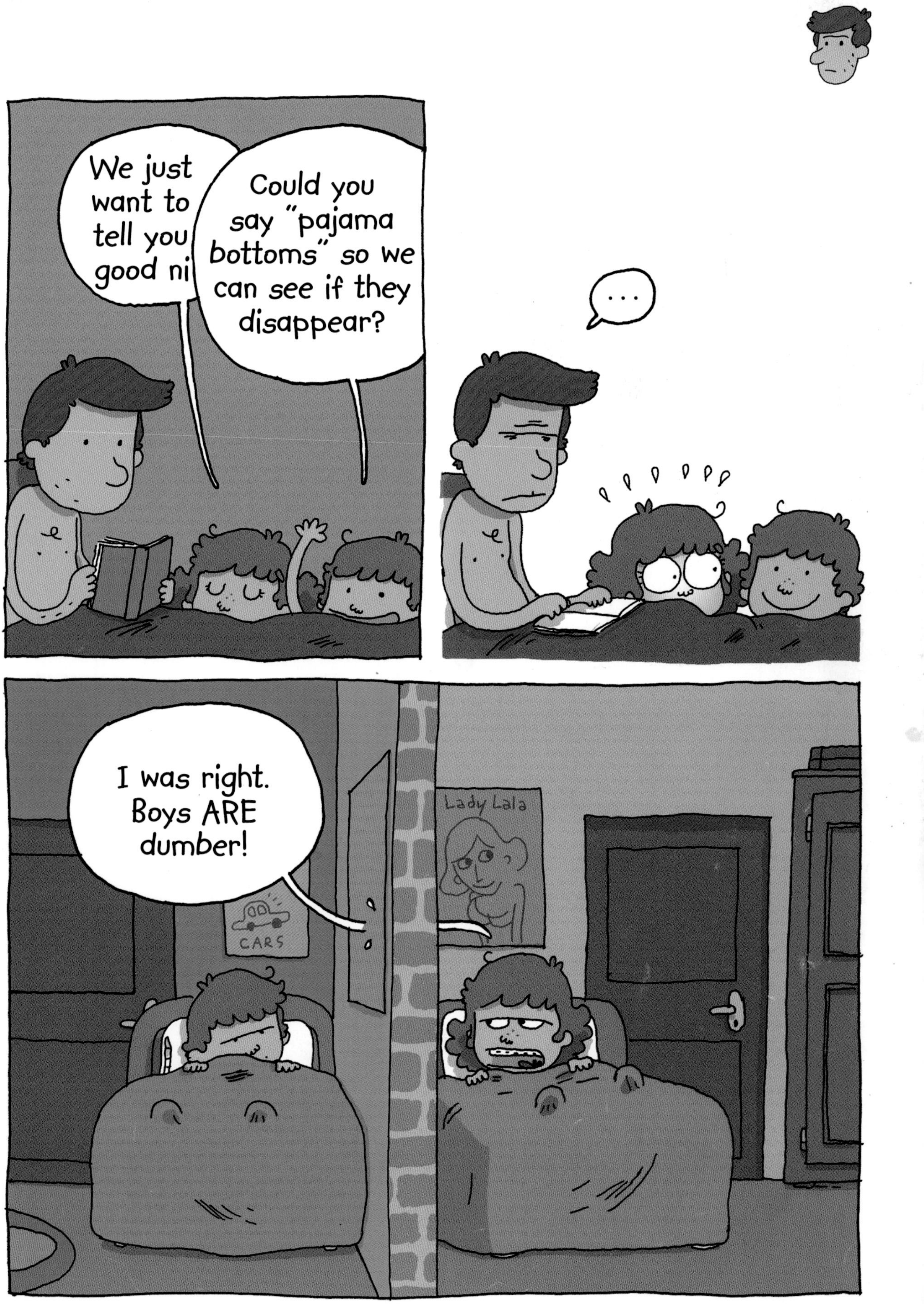
We just want to tell you good ni
Could you say "pajama bottoms" so we can see if they disappear?
...
I was right. Boys ARE dumber!
CARS
Lady Lala

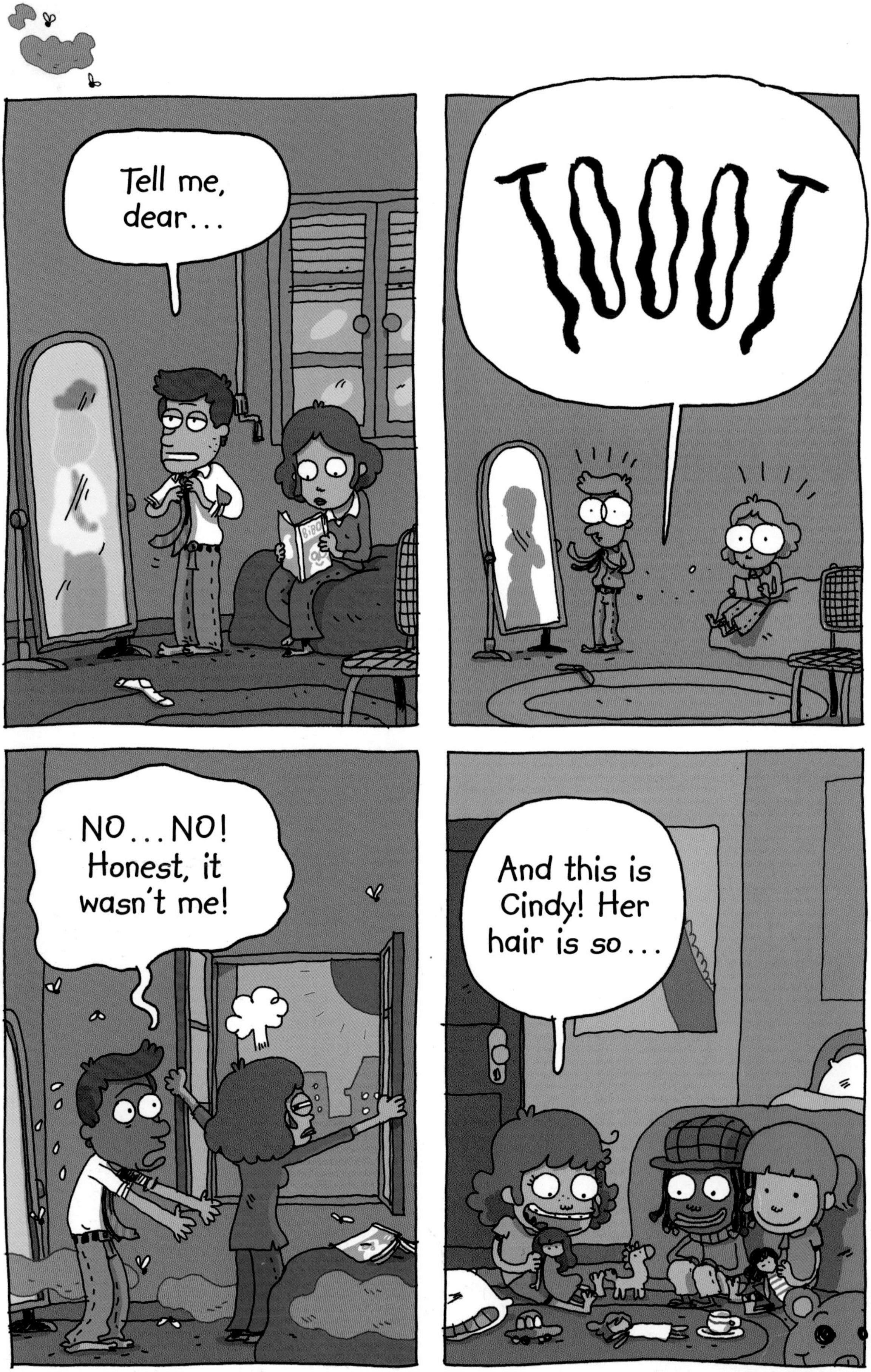
Tell me, dear...
TOOOT
NO...NO! Honest, it wasn't me!
And this is Cindy! Her hair is so...

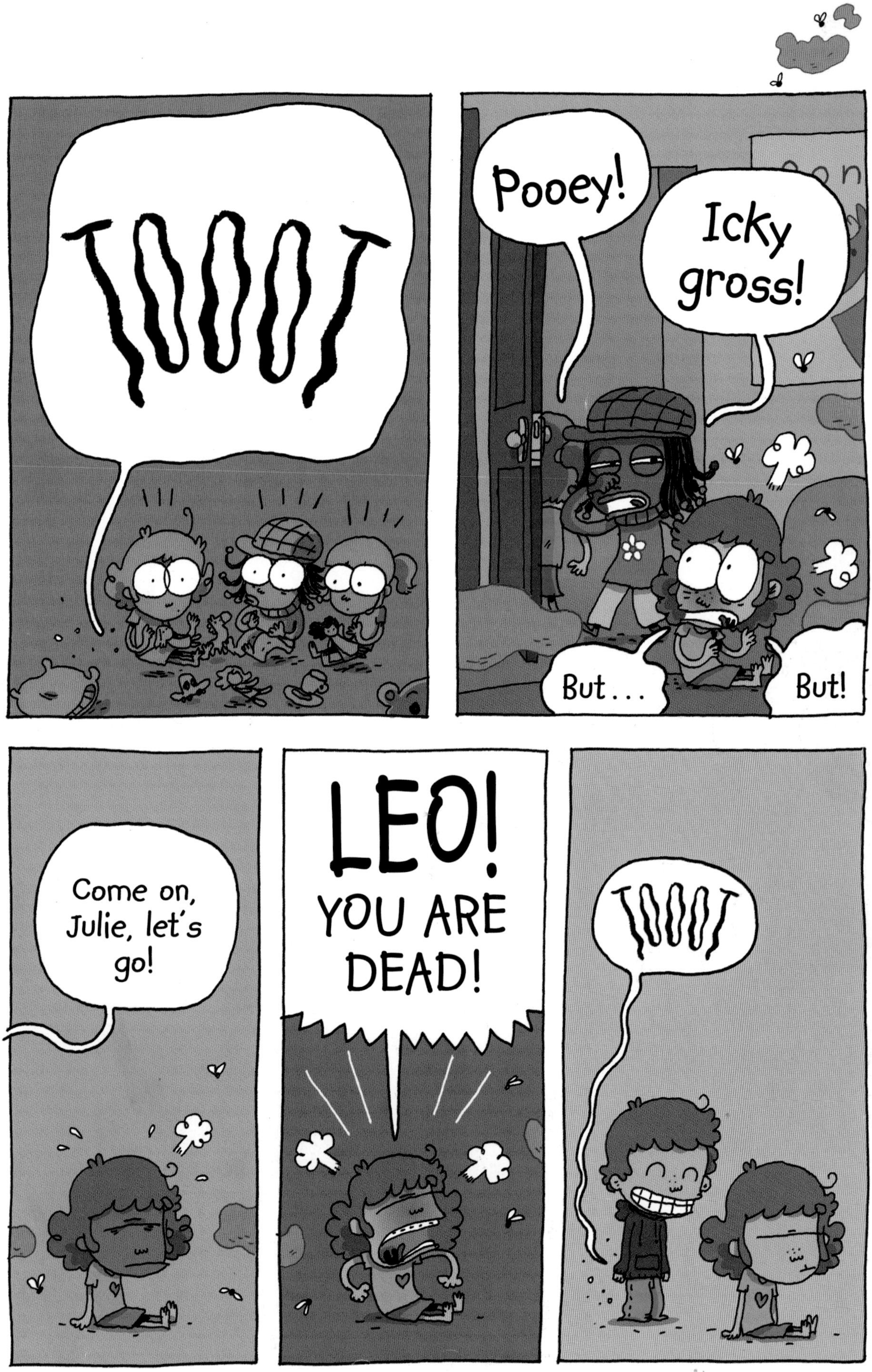
TOOOT
Pooey!
Icky gross!
But...
But!
Come on, Julie, let's go!
LEO! YOU ARE DEAD!
TOOOT

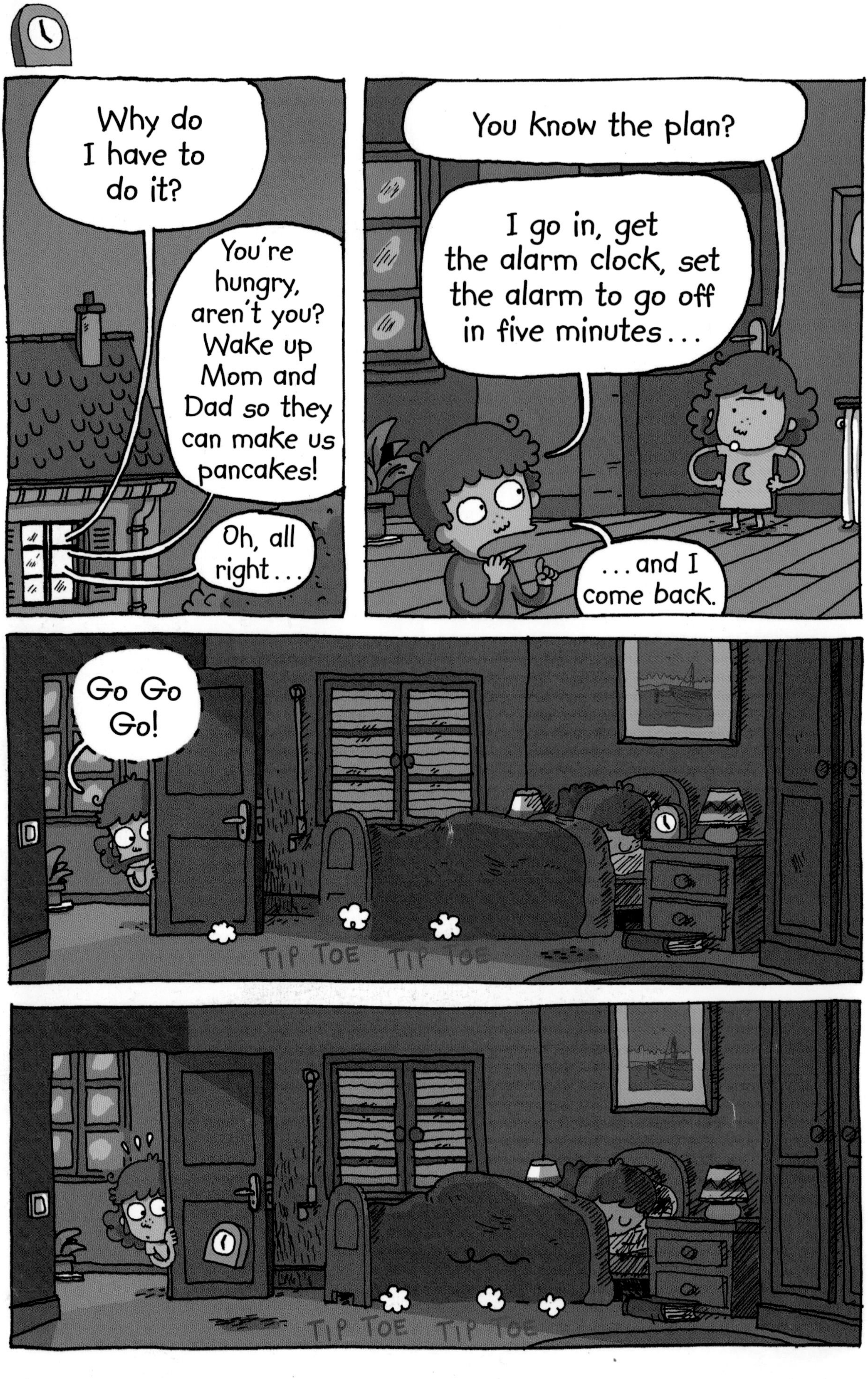

Why do I have to do it?
You're hungry, aren't you? Wake up Mom and Dad so they can make us pancakes!
Oh, all right...
You know the plan?
I go in, get the alarm clock, set the alarm to go off in five minutes...
...and I come back.
Go Go Go!
TIP TOE TIP TOE
TIP TOE TIP TOE

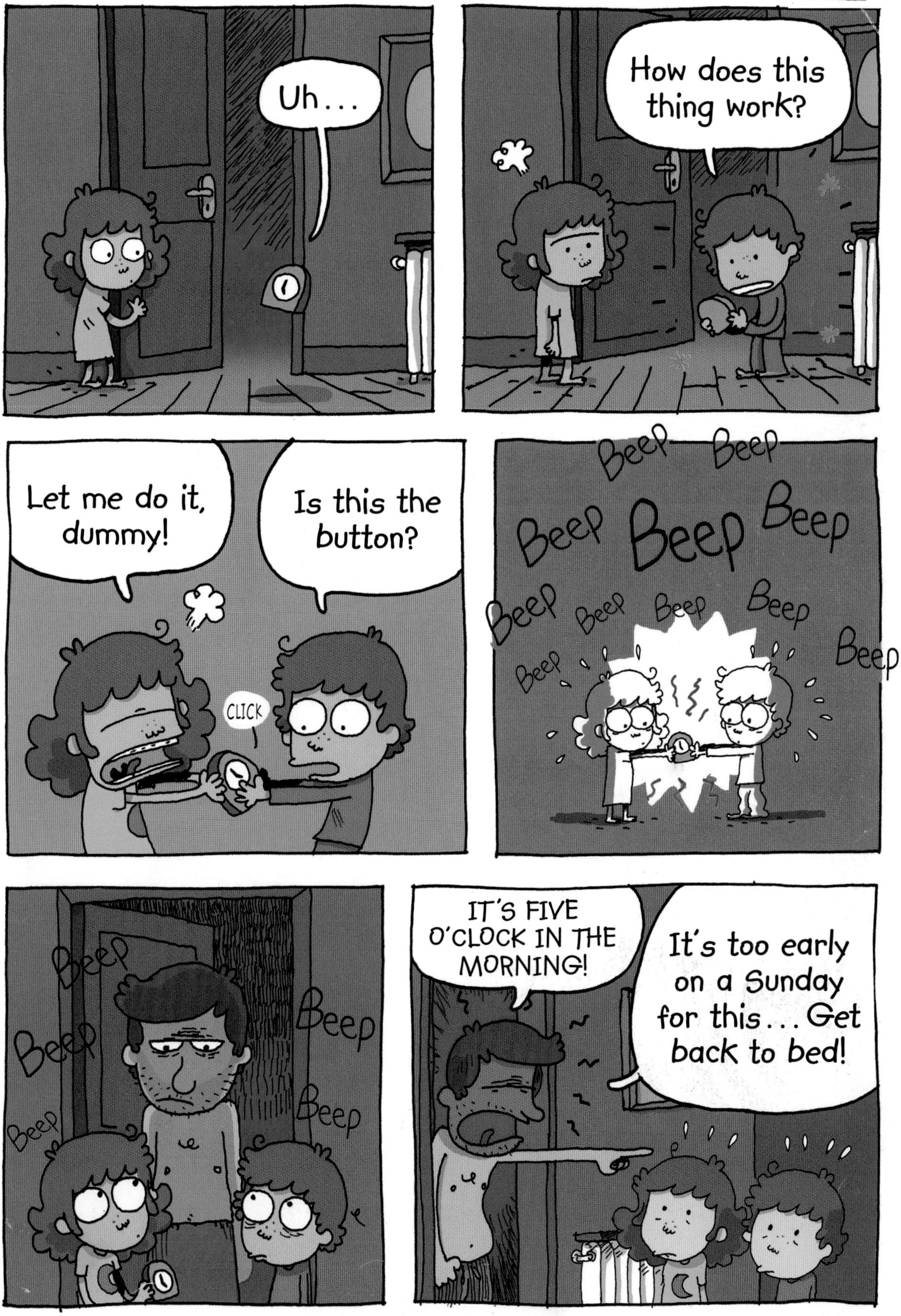
Uh...
How does this thing work?
Let me do it, dummy!
Is this the button?
CLICK
Beep Beep
Beep Beep Beep
Beep Beep Beep Beep
Beep Beep
Beep
Beep
Beep
Beep
IT'S FIVE O'CLOCK IN THE MORNING!
It's too early on a Sunday for this... Get back to bed!

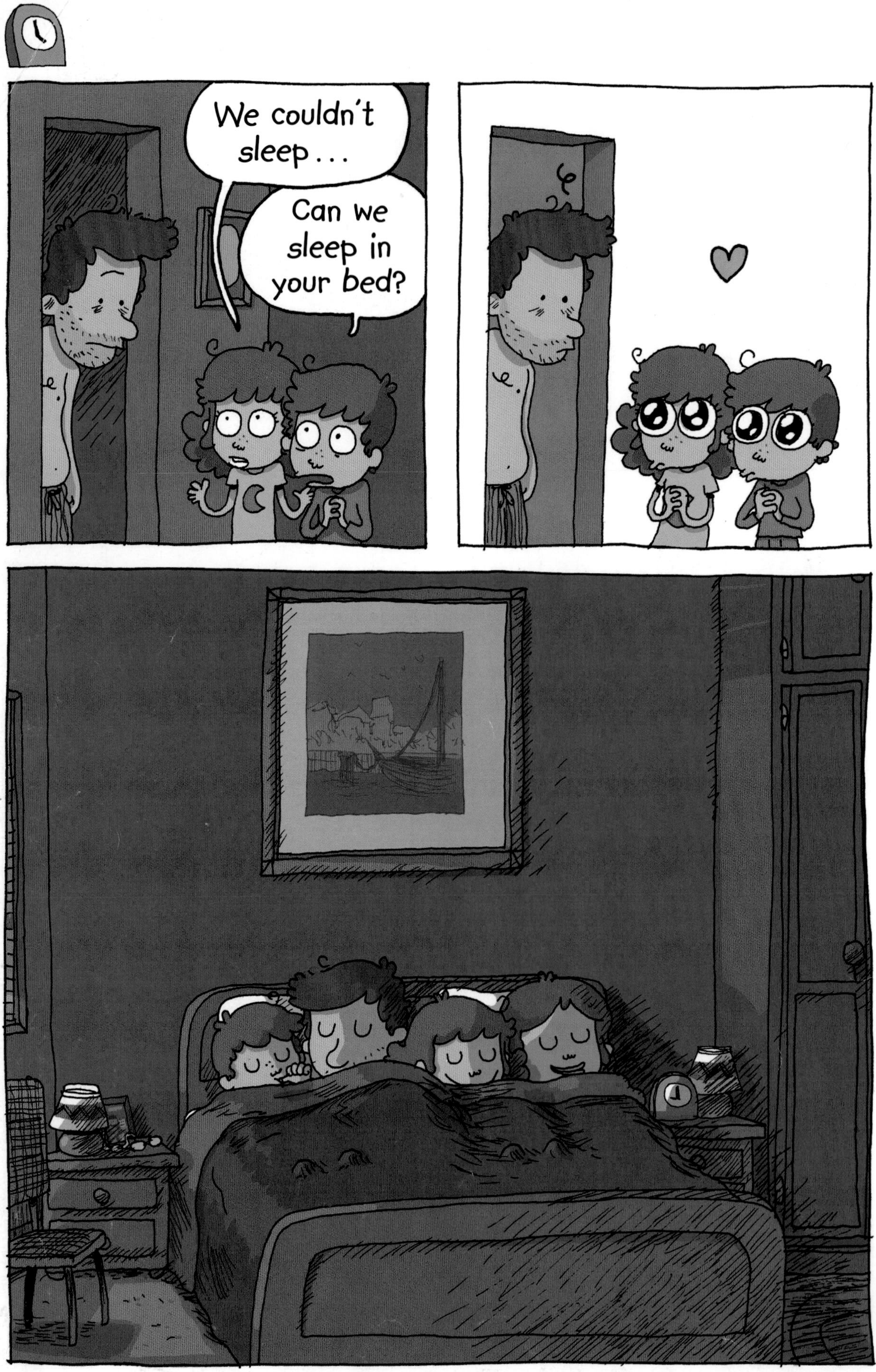

We couldn't sleep...
Can we sleep in your bed?

THE END

Readers! Can you find 12 THINGS that Leopold has sneakily moved or taken away?

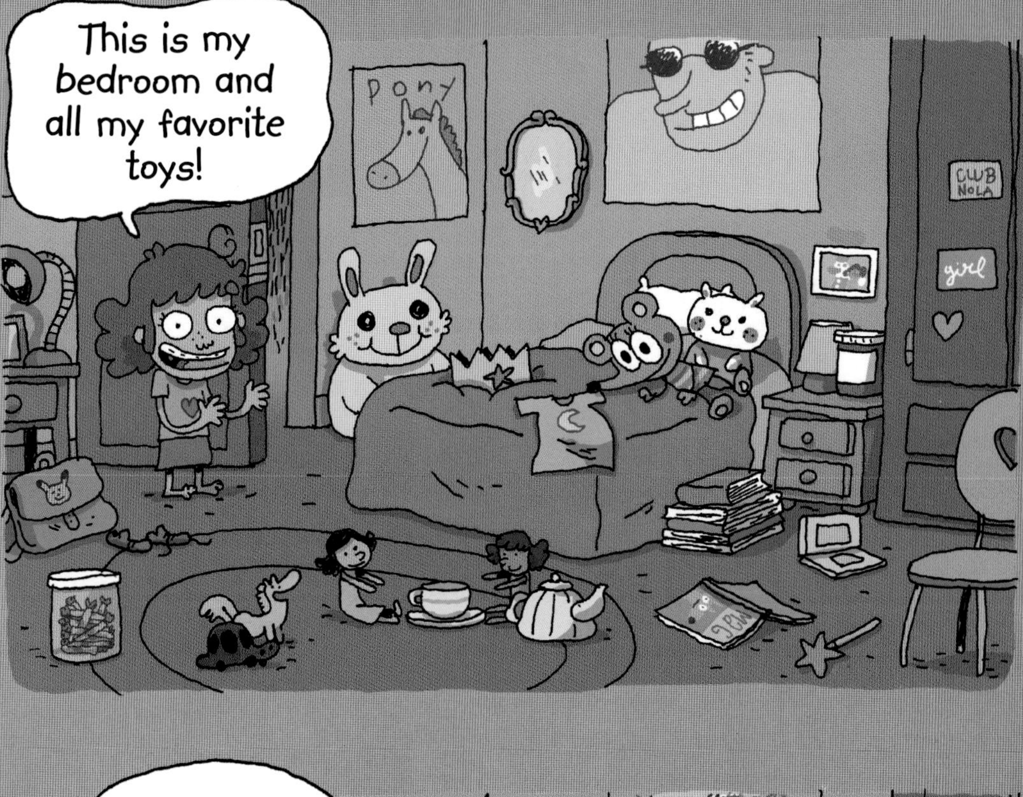
This is my bedroom and all my favorite toys!
PONY
CLUB NOLA
girl

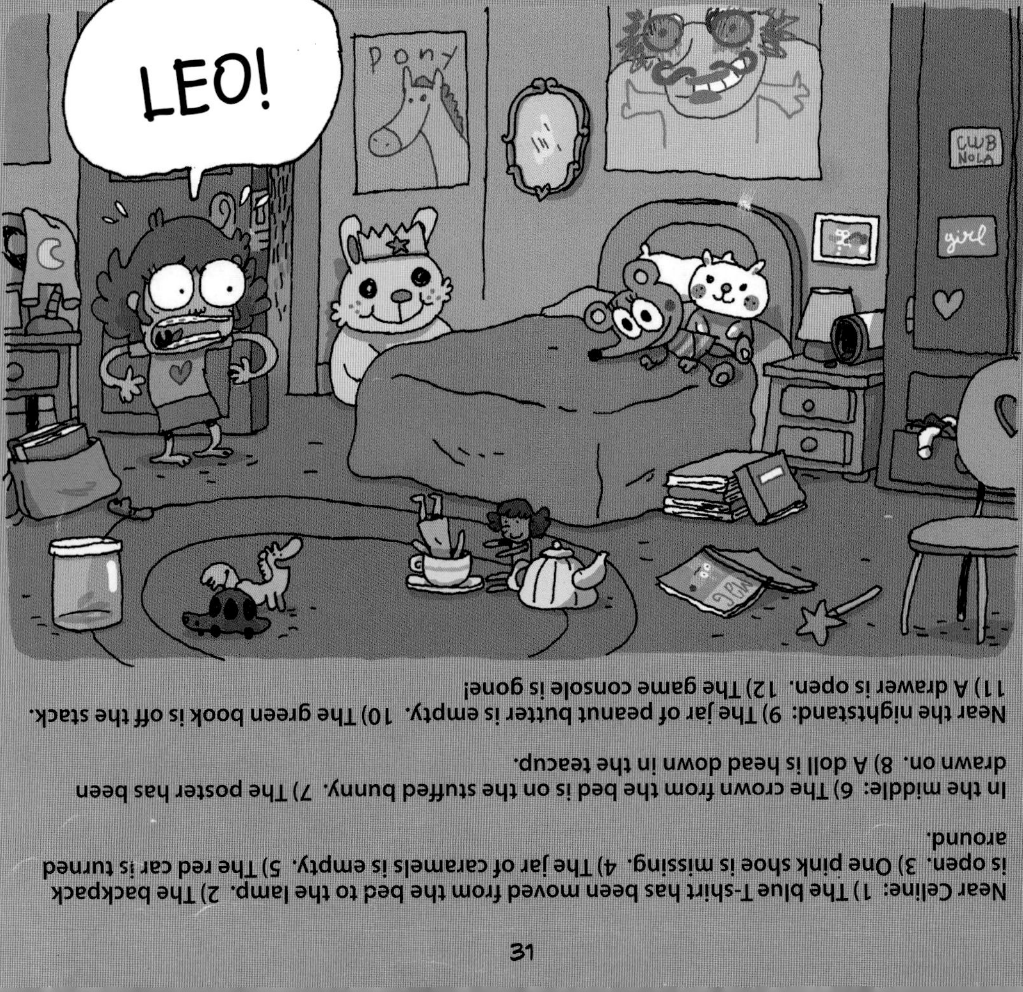
LEO!
PONY
CLUB NOLA
girl

Near Celine: 1) The blue T-shirt has been moved from the bed to the lamp. 2) The backpack is open. 3) One pink shoe is missing. 4) The jar of caramels is empty. 5) The red car is turned around.

In the middle: 6) The crown from the bed is on the stuffed bunny. 7) The poster has been drawn on. 8) A doll is head down in the teacup.

Near the nightstand: 9) The jar of peanut butter is empty. 10) The green book is off the stack. 11) A drawer is open. 12) The game console is gone!

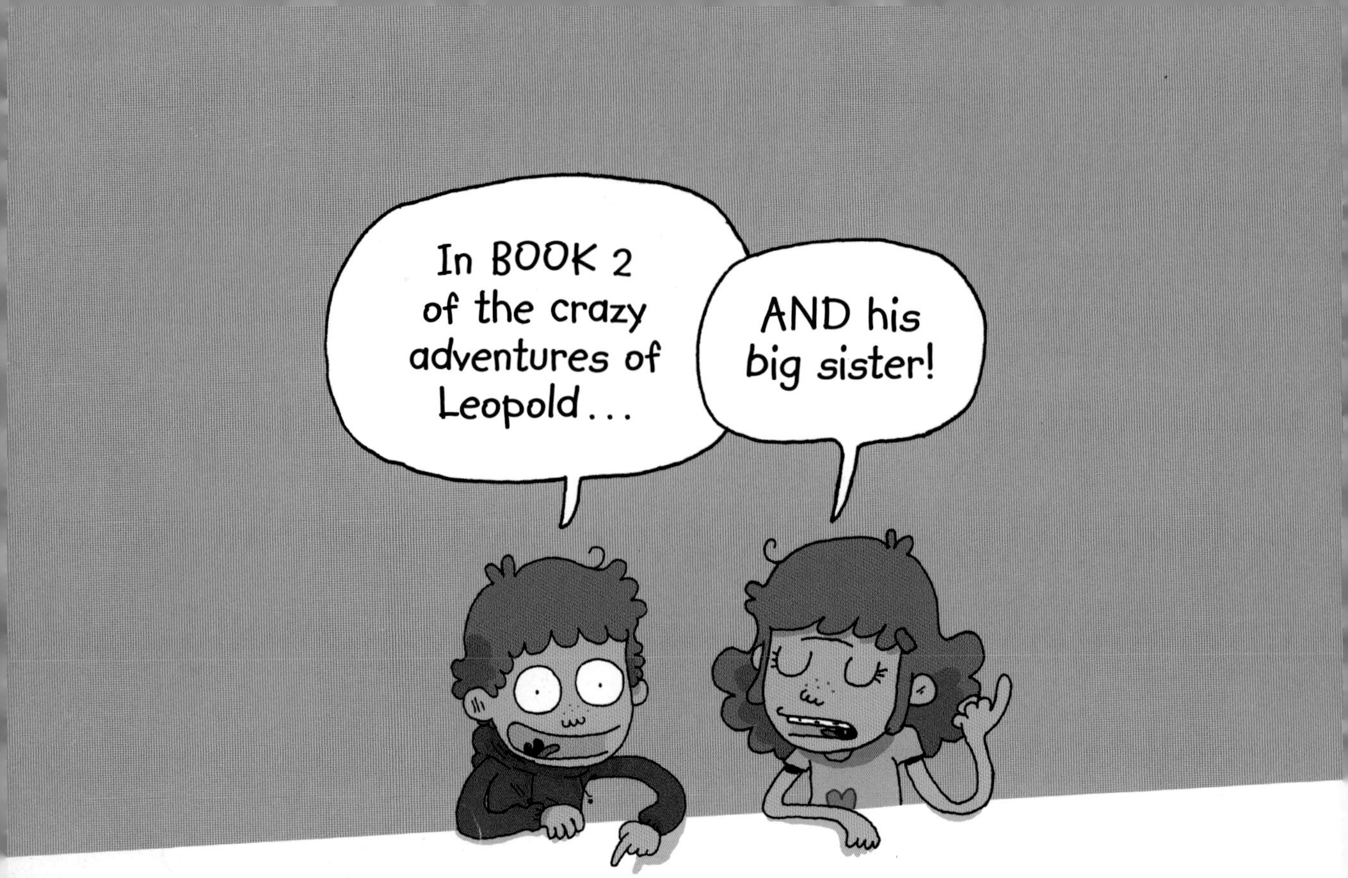
In BOOK 2 of the crazy adventures of Leopold...
AND his big sister!

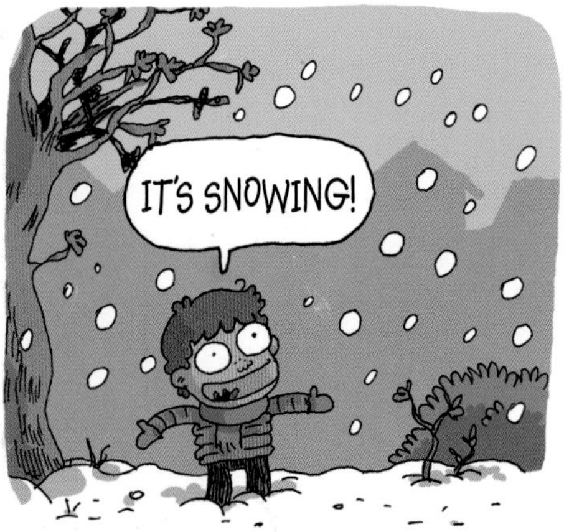
IT'S SNOWING!

Surprises!

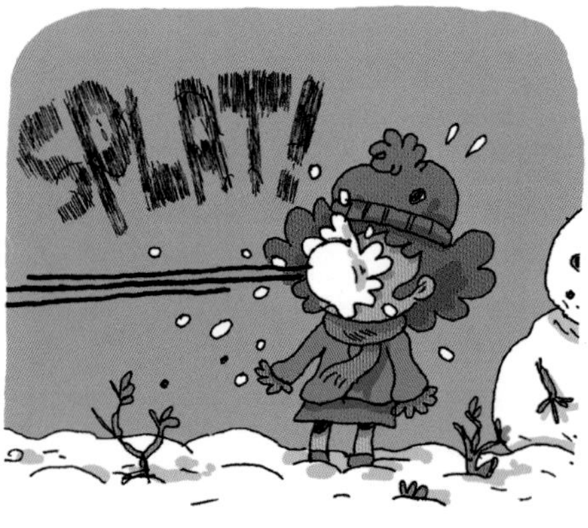
SPLAT!

Laughs!

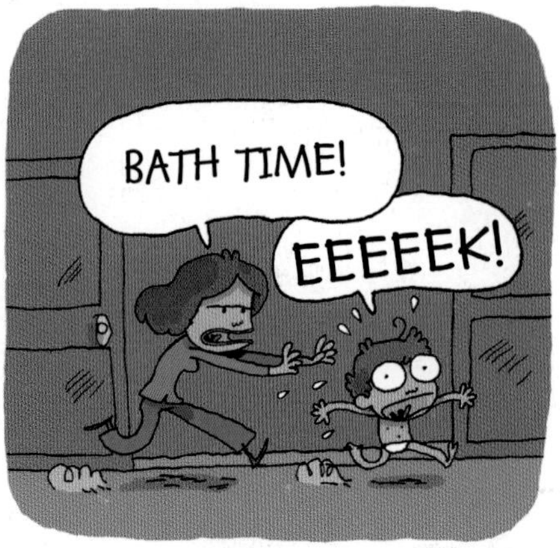
BATH TIME!
EEEEEK!

Danger!

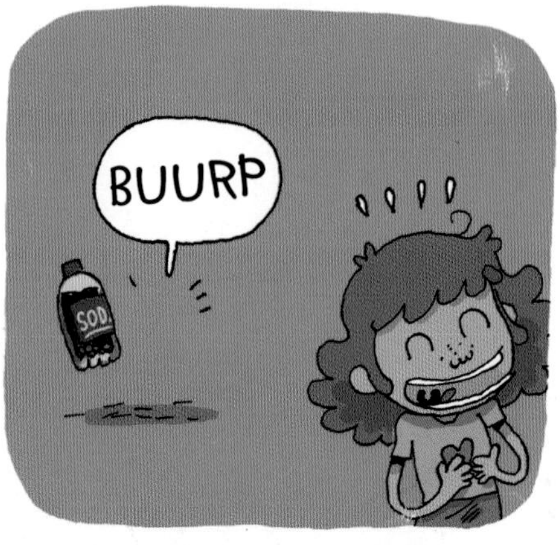
BUURP
SOD.

...And lots of jokes!

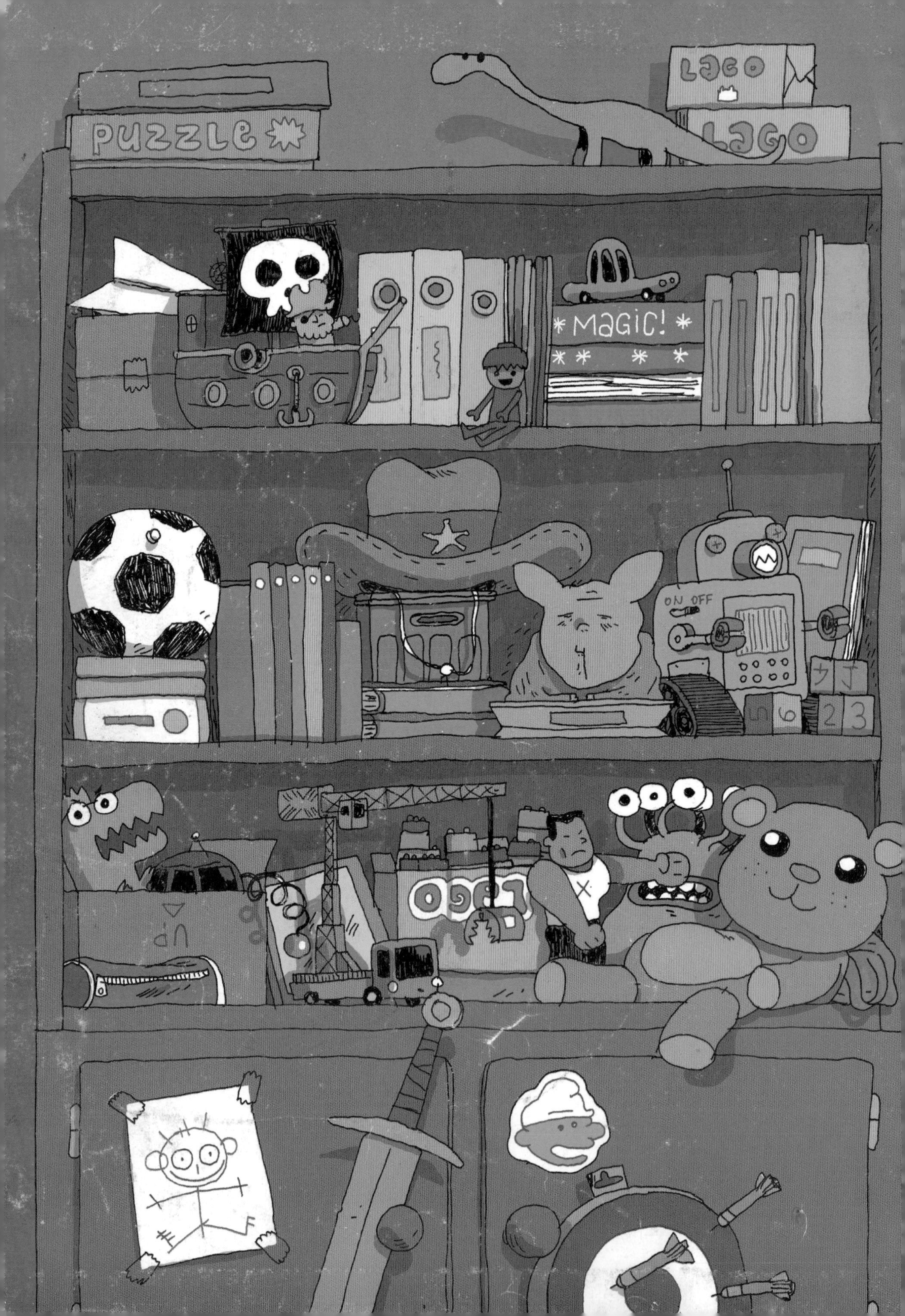
PUZZLE
LAGO
LAGO
MAGIC!
ON OFF